# FLO AND MAUDE SAVE A SANTA

SARAH OSBORNE

**BOOKS BY SARAH OSBORNE**

Ditie Brown Mysteries

*Too Many Crooks Spoil the Plot*

*Into the Frying Pan*

*Murder Most Southern*

*The House of Good and Evil*

Flo and Maude Christmas Cozies

*Flo and Maude Christmas Capers*

*Flo and Maude Save a Santa*

# FLO AND MAUDE SAVE A SANTA

This book is a work of fiction Names, characters, places, and incidents are products of the author's imagination or are used fictitiously. Any resemblance to actual events or locales or persons living or dead is entirely coincidental.



First Edition: November 2021

ISBN: 978-1-7375565-4-1

Imprint: Independently published

Printed in the United States of America

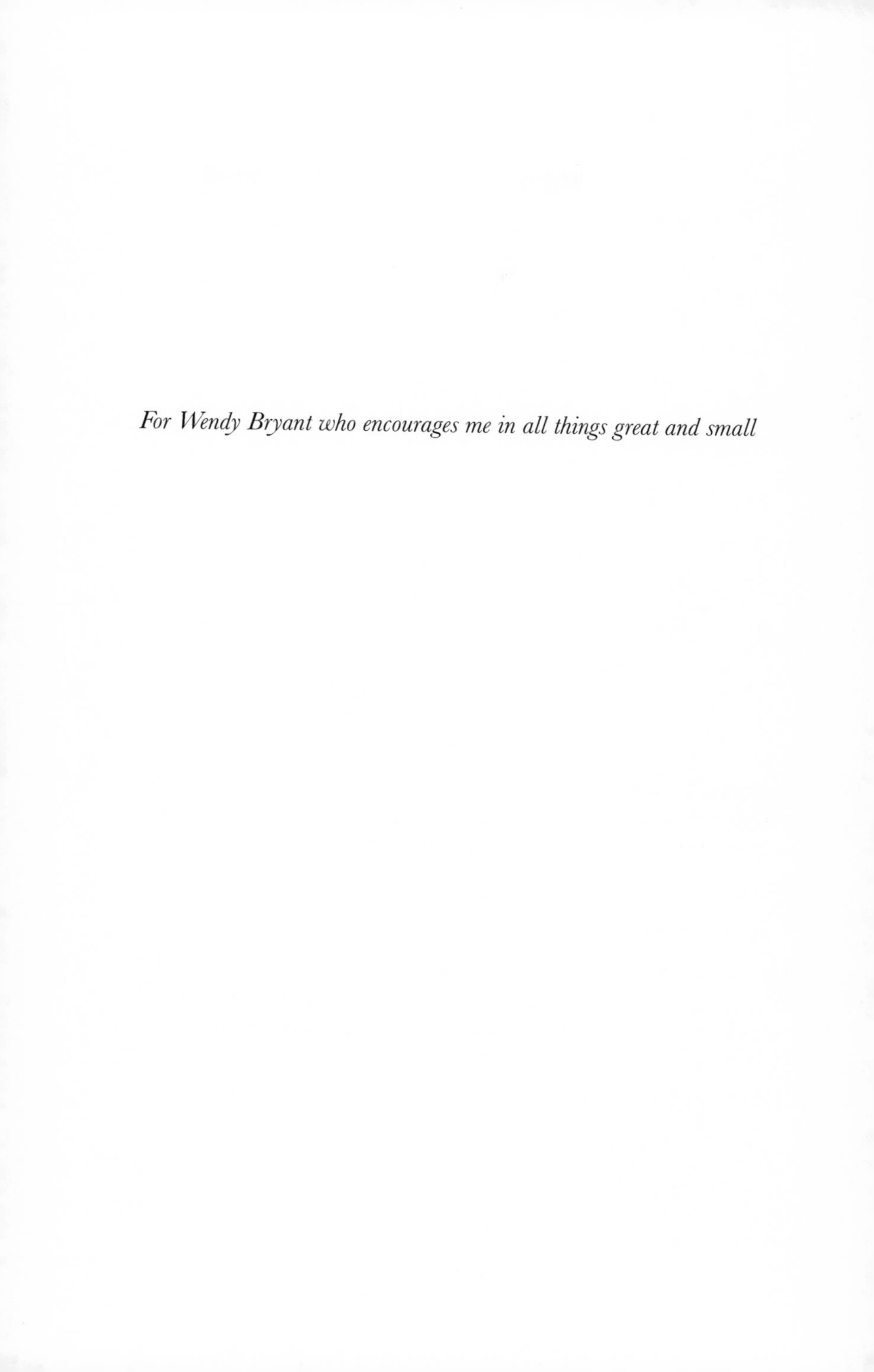

*For Wendy Bryant who encourages me in all things great and small*

# ACKNOWLEDGMENTS

My first thank you must go, as it always does, to my conscientious beta readers: Jayne Farley, Kathy McCarthy, Mary Louise Klimm, Laurie Pocius, Lynne Rozsa, Margo Schmidt, and Donna Shapiro. They are the people who tell me frankly what works and doesn't work in my mystery. Without them I would be lost.

My exercise group—241 Fitness headed by Wendy Bryant—offer me encouragement to keep my mind and body in shape.

Aisha Akeju designs beautiful covers for me. I'm very lucky to have her on board.

Finally, I continue to thrive with the love of support of Dan and Alix.

# 1

"It's December and we have no plans for Christmas," I said. "No one has called our agency desperate for protection." I picked up my fork and poked around the left-over beef stew that was supposed to be my supper. Then I put my fork down again.

Kate paused between bites of what she apparently found delicious. "Flo, you say that every year, and someone in danger always turns up.

"Are you our cheerleader now?" I asked. "That's more Maude's job."

I knew I was being snarky. I got that way when I was bored or hungry. Today, I was both. Marianne, our cook, had taken the evening off, so we were left to forage for ourselves and find whatever leftovers we wanted to eat.

I didn't care for leftovers.

I also didn't care for constant rain. Even inside my Boston brownstone with its thick walls, I could hear the rain pounding on the pavement outside. It sounded as if one of those therapy drumming groups had decided to set up camp on our doorstep.

I sighed and looked out the dining room window.

The street was dark. Lamps yielded small circles of light with limp garlands hanging from each one. Chronic rain made me irritable. Some people might say I didn't need rain to make me grouchy. I preferred to think of myself as someone with discerning taste and a clear vision of what she liked and didn't like.

"So gloomy out there," I said, "and wet. I'm ready for snow! Where can we go to find a dependable white Christmas?"

"Switzerland?" Kate asked.

This time *Kate* was being snarky. She knew my secret—that I hated to fly—but occasionally she couldn't help herself.

"How about Maine?" Maude asked.

She was the one I could count on for good suggestions. She was a tad older than I was—maybe eighty-five—we didn't discuss age much. She was sharp as a tack, and truth be told, she was gentler than either Kate or I tended to be.

Kate and I weren't family, but we could have been. We were both independent and forthright. People often accused me of being too direct. Honestly, how can you be too direct if you are simply telling the truth or stating the obvious? They never complained about Kate who was equally outspoken—probably because she was a strikingly beautiful woman in her early forties. She could get away with murder, so to speak.

We'd met years ago after I saw her in an Olympics biathlon event—that weird event where people cross-country ski and shoot at targets. Kate needed a job, and I needed someone to protect me from harm. That's what my father said shortly before he died. He told me he wanted to know someone would be looking out for me when he couldn't be my bodyguard anymore.

I almost laughed at that—I'd always looked out for myself. But I was too sad to laugh. Dad was failing, and I wasn't sure how I'd cope without him. I honored his request. It turned out to be one of the best decisions I ever made—or perhaps to put it more accurately—one of the best decisions my father ever made.

Kate understood me. She knew when to leave me to my own devices, but she also knew when I needed her. And she was good with numbers. I hated worrying about bills and estate issues. Kate seemed to thrive on those concerns. "It's all about focus," she told me, "and accuracy. It's what I do when I'm shooting. It's the same with financial matters—you keep your eye on the details and everything else falls into place."

Maude and I met years later when I rescued her from a person intent on murdering her. That, however, is another story.

Kate, Maude and I had different talents. I liked to think of myself as the one who offered direction and often solutions to the problems we found. Maude supplied the sweetness and warmth when needed. People told her their life stories whenever she asked. She could open up a can of tuna and get it to reveal when it had last been swimming in the ocean. Kate kept us safe. She could shoot and ski with the best of them. In our line of work there wasn't much call for cross-country skiing, but we sometimes needed quick action and accuracy when it came to using a gun.

What we had in common was our love of adventure and our desire to rescue people who found themselves in danger—hence our highly successful "ODPA: Old Dames Protection Agency."

I suppose highly successful was dependent on how one measured things. We were close to breaking even this year in terms of money earned and money spent, not that that was my highest priority. As a Boston Brahmin, my father had left me enough money to do whatever I wanted with my life. But the IRS called my detective agency a "hobby," and *that* I found extremely insulting. Only when we started turning a profit would we become a reputable business in its eyes.

Kate was an honorary member of ODPA—too young to be official—but she *was* our official business manager. She liked to say we were inching toward solvency. People promised to pay us for protection, but once they were out of danger, they often forgot they owed us money. Kate made sure everyone signed a contract if they wanted *her* services, and that meant more money flowed into our bank account this year than last. She did a lot of smaller jobs for people who needed protection while I waited for a big assignment every Christmas. So far one had turned up on our doorstep each December since we'd formed our agency.

Solvency had a nice ring to it, but I liked Maude's definition of success better. "Think of the lives we've saved!" Kate always had to add her two cents to that discussion. "Most of them worth saving, I suppose."

I'd been floating in nostalgia, but I came back to the present.

"What will we do *this* Christmas?" I asked.

Maude took her plate to the kitchen and returned with her iPad. She smiled as she opened it. "Flo, I've just heard from a mutual friend of ours. Her daughter lives outside Portland, Maine, and the daughter has a neighbor who may be in serious trouble. Ida is afraid the neighbor will be harmed, possibly killed if we don't intervene."

"Ida? A mutual friend?" I said. "The name is vaguely familiar."

"Should be," Maude said. "She was a classmate at Radcliffe and she certainly remembers you after what you did."

"What I did?"

"You wanted to show her that her boyfriend was no good, so you threw yourself at him, and he responded. Ida found him embracing you in the lobby of her dorm."

"Ah, yes, that Ida. I kept her from a life of misery."

"Yes," Maude said, "and humiliated her in front of her friends."

"She wouldn't take my word for it," I said, "so I figured seeing is believing."

"Actually, she says she now appreciates what you did. She's married to a wonderful man although it took her years to trust men again."

"She can't blame me for that," I said. "A lot of men aren't trustworthy."

"Is that why you never married, Flo?" Kate asked.

"No. Like you I love my freedom, and I'm not good at compromise."

"And you never regretted that decision?" Kate asked.

I thought about that for a moment. "No. I had a lot of tumbles in the hay, enough anyway, so no, I don't regret anything about my life."

Maude turned back to the email. "Ida said she read about our successes in the book you self-published, Flo."

"Must you call it my self-published book? Couldn't you call it by its proper name—*Flo and Maude Christmas Capers*? Couldn't you mention how well received it was?"

Kate chuckled. "Two hundred copies sold—probably sold to friends who owed you favors."

Kate must have seen she'd hurt my feelings. She shook out her thick black hair and twisted it back in a bun. "I have to say, Flo, you did a good job with that book. Very true to our adventures. I guess I'm as bored as you are, so let's hear about the daughter's neighbor who may be in trouble."

"Does the neighbor have a name?" I asked.

"Bob Quellette," Maude said.

"What an unusual last name," I said.

"Not in Maine. I trained with a lot of skiers in Maine,"

Kate said. "Many of them had French-Canadian names like Quellette."

"And the daughter's name?" I asked.

"Cora," Maude said. "I saw a lot of Cora growing up, but I never met her husband, Charlie. She seemed to keep him under wraps for some reason, and there was no grand wedding. Ida and I lost touch over the last twenty years except for an occasional Christmas card."

"Cora and Charlie are eager for us to come?" I asked.

"Ida doesn't say. She simply says her daughter has room for the three of us and that it's urgent we get there as soon as possible. Ida plans to visit her son, but she won't feel happy about leaving until we arrive. She promises to pay all our expenses."

"Maybe you should read the email aloud," Kate said.

Kate and I pushed our dishes to one side and sat at the dining room table, leaning forward to hear Maude's quiet voice over the pelting rain outside.

*"Hi dear Maude, I'm so sorry about the troubles in your life—divorcing your husband and losing your daughter. In your last Christmas card you sounded as if you were finding joy in life once more, and I am so happy to hear that. With Flo Wellington, no less."*

"What does that mean?" I asked.

"Perhaps if you let her read the whole email without interrupting," Kate said, "we could hear what it means."

"Go on," I said and popped a chocolate peppermint in my mouth to keep it closed for a while.

Maude cleared her throat and ran a hand over her short white hair.

*"As to Flo, I know she did me a favor that kept me from marrying a terrible man, but she did it in such a harsh way. Then again, that's who Flo has always been—direct and to the point. Now, I think she's finally found her niche. You, too, it seems. I've read about the amazing success of your agency in preventing murders.*

*"That's why I'm writing. I'm terribly worried about my daughter's neighbor, Bob Quellette. He doesn't see the need for you, but I do. I've been staying with Cora for a few weeks. She and her husband, Charlie, have a small farm northeast of Portland outside the town of Menescotta."*

This time it was Kate who interrupted. "Menescotta? I had an old boyfriend there. It's a darling town."

"What is it, dear?" Maude asked. "You sound wistful."

Kate shook her head. "It's nothing. He was a sweetie. I've wondered sometimes if I gave up on that relationship too soon."

Something clicked into place for me. Kate had asked me how satisfied I was with my life. Maybe it was because she wasn't satisfied with her own. This wasn't the time to discuss that, but we would. Later. It might also explain why Kate had seemed so out of sorts recently. Negative. That wasn't like her. That was more like me.

Maude looked at both of us. I nodded, and she continued to read.

*"Bob lives half a mile away from my daughter on his own small farm. He's a dear man—to me anyway—and I see him every time I'm in town. My daughter claims I catch him on his good days, especially during the holiday season. Otherwise, she says he's more of a recluse, but when he puts on his Santa suit he becomes a warm outgoing fellow. He's been Menescotta's Santa in the big Christmas parade for at least fifteen years, but this year he says he can't be Santa.*

*"It's not what you might think. It's not an age or health problem. Bob is in his mid-sixties. He's a perfect chubby Santa complete with an authentic beard. He told me his decision had nothing to do with his general health. He said someone didn't want him to play Santa Claus anymore. I think it's more serious than that. I think Bob should be in fear of his life."*

"In fear of his life?" I said. A peppermint patty could keep me silent only so long. "A Santa in fear of his life?"

"Let me finish, Flo," Maude said. "I'm almost done."

*"Bob wouldn't tell me more. He said he didn't know more really. He*

*said when he went to get his Santa costume out of moth balls, it was ripped to shreds. His Santa boots were covered in paint. The bag he used to bring presents to the village center was full of torn paper—newspaper. They were old articles from the Menescotta Press, and he couldn't make sense of them. They were all from several years past."*

"Couldn't make sense of them or didn't want to make sense of them?" I asked.

Maude shook her head. "Ida doesn't know but she wonders if there was something Bob wasn't telling her. She finishes up the email by asking if we can stay with her daughter, Cora, and look into things. She's very worried about Bob, and she wants the town's Santa to remain safe and sound."

"Let's get our bags packed," I said. "Tell her we're on our way."

Maude looked at me. I could read every expression on her face, and this time she gave me a sheepish grin. "I told her we'd be arriving in two days."

## 2

"Two days?" I said. "Can we manage that?"

Maude's smile broadened. "I thought you'd be annoyed I hadn't said tomorrow."

"It's only three hours from here, maybe less," Kate said. "We could go tomorrow. You can get Natalie to take care of things here."

"It would give her something to do," I said, "other than dance around to Zumba music and pretend she's cleaning the house." Natalie was my housekeeper, probably a more accurate description would be my house-observer. She liked to know what was going on and only rarely felt the need to dust or keep things in order.

I looked at Maude. "This will be perfect. I hope we don't solve this problem too quickly and have to come back to dreary Boston before Christmas."

"Ida said we could stay as long as we wanted," Maude said, "and that her daughter wouldn't mind a bit. Being out in the countryside will do us all good."

"You don't have a boyfriend, Kate, who wants to see you at Christmas?" I asked.

"Menescotta is three hours away. Anyone who wants to see me can make the drive."

We were ready to leave the next morning. We hadn't put out any Christmas decorations yet, so we didn't have to worry about that. Natalie was delighted with the prospect of a week or more without us.

"No wild parties," I told her. "My neighbors will keep me informed."

She gave me that nod that could mean almost anything. She'd probably invite the neighbors so they'd keep their mouths shut. And Marianne, our cook, would undoubtedly prepare a magnificent feast for anyone who wished to come. Honestly, that was fine with me. I wanted an adventure, and if others enjoyed themselves while I was gone, good for them.

Maude called Ida who said it was a fine thing we were coming early. She needed to leave immediately, and she wasn't sure Bob would make it through the next week without harm. The strangest things were happening at his farm. He'd tripped over a hoe that had been left outside and he'd suffered a black eye. According to Ida, Bob was fastidious. Nothing was left out of place, and everything was always in perfect working order. Yet, somehow he'd tripped over a hoe left in the middle of his front yard because his outside lights hadn't come on.

I secretly wondered if Bob was a drinker, but that could wait until we met him. We left mid-morning. The drive to Portland, our first stop, was an easy one on four- and six-lane roads most of the way. Snow-covered pine trees lined the sides of the road and traffic was light.

We stopped in Portland at a restaurant Kate had recommended, called Slab Sicilian Street Food. She said it had excellent craft beer and pizza. Those were two of my guilty pleasures and not something I would allow myself to be seen eating or drinking in Boston. There is no way to look refined with a beer in front of you and pizza in your mouth. But, oh, the food and beer were delicious.

The roads were clear as we left Portland and headed northeast. Gently rolling hills were covered in fresh snow, and the area grew more and more rural, particularly as we neared Menescotta. Mixed forests lined the wide highway: beech, birch, white pine and spruce firs. I didn't know any of the names but Maude did. "So many species," she said with excitement. "Did you know, Flo, Maine has more forests than any other state in the Union?"

I didn't know that, but I did know the trees were gorgeous with the new snow on their branches. If I were one to wax poetic I'd say we'd entered a winter wonderland.

Maude did it for me. "Look at all of this—blue sky, clean white snow everywhere. Did you see the red barn with its snow-covered roof? It looked just like a picture postcard. I wonder what cows do in weather like this?"

"They hide," Kate said, "and the snow won't stay clean for long."

Maude was sitting in the back. She reached up and patted Kate's arm. "It's beautiful for now, dear, and isn't this Barbara Ross country—where she sets her Maine Clambake Mystery series?"

"It is," Kate said.

Kate and Maude kept up with all the cozy mystery writers in New England and beyond. I preferred to get my mysteries in the flesh, so to speak.

"She sets her stories right on the coast," Kate said. "Menescotta is on a river nearby. It feeds into the ocean near the harbor she writes about. Oysters are farmed from the river and once a year alewives run and spawn in that river. It's amazing to witness!"

"Alewives?" I asked. "Isn't that something you'd see in a local pub?"

"Fish," Kate said, "used as lobster bait."

"How do you know so much about the area?" Maude asked.

"I knew a fisherman once." Kate stopped speaking as abruptly as she'd started.

Maude didn't press for more information, and I settled back to enjoy the view. We drove through the town of Menescotta—signaled by a small bridge over the river Kate had told us about. Main Street was lined with two dozen shops and restaurants.

"Lovely," Maude said.

The house address we had for Cora took us back into the countryside on Route 1. The elevation increased, and at times it felt as if we were on a roller coaster. In the distance we could see hills covered in snow. Small farms dotted the landscape. Some houses stood off from the road with cleared land surrounding them. We occasionally saw a few animals outside a barn—a horse, some goats, a cow.

The road was now two lanes instead of four. The farms were tucked in and surrounded by forest on either side. A small barn of weathering cedar often stood near the main house or occasionally attached to it. The barns were mostly small and functional. Some had cupolas on top and a mansard roof. All were practical, Kate told us. The cupolas kept air flowing inside the barn, and the mansard roofs kept the snow from sticking.

Sometimes we saw open fields, but it was clear that land would revert to forest if left untouched by human hands. There was a wild feel to much of it. The farmers here had their work cut out for them—hearty New England farmers who had to cultivate the land simply to keep it from vanishing into forest.

I smiled.

We weren't in Boston anymore. We were in another universe—one that was rugged and pristine. Best of all it held a mystery to solve and a life to save.

I looked over at Kate to see if she was feeling the same way I was. She remained focused on the road ahead, her mouth in a thin line. I wondered again what might be bothering her.

We arrived at Cora and Charlie's around five in the afternoon. It was already getting dark. Their farm was set off from the road, and Kate drove us carefully up a long drive that led to the main house. The drive had been partially cleared but not snowplowed. A porch extended along the front and sides of the two-story white clapboard house. It was just the house I would have wanted if I ever thought I could live in the country—which I couldn't.

The porch railing was wrapped in garland, and a wreath decorated with red ribbon and pine cones hung over the door knocker. No Christmas lights covered the roof line as we'd seen on many of the farms we'd passed.

Before we could knock, a woman opened the door. She looked to be in her fifties, but I was no longer a good judge of age. Everyone I saw looked young. This had to be Cora and she greeted us warmly. She had a softness about her that reminded me of Maude with a warm smile and large brown eyes that assured us we were welcome.

She ushered us inside.

"My mom had to leave this morning to make sure she could get to my brother's—he lives in the Midwest, and a winter storm is brewing there. She's so sorry to miss you. This is my husband, Charlie."

Charlie was affable but less talkative. He was a good-looking man in a rugged sort of way, wearing glasses, a cap, a work shirt, boots and a heavy coat. "I'll bring in your bags and then I've got to check on the animals before it gets too dark. I'll be back in time to help with dinner."

Cora gave him a funny look. Once he was gone, she turned to us. "Charlie never helps with dinner. I think he wanted to make a good impression on you. I don't mind—I love to cook."

She helped us out of our winter coats and held the door open when Charlie returned with three small suitcases.

"You travel light," Cora said.

"I didn't think we'd be going out on the town," I said. "Will we?"

"Oh no," Cora laughed. "We might go into town, but we are a small farming and fishing community. We don't dress up even for church."

Kate offered to help Charlie with the bags.

"No need, I got it." He headed upstairs.

"You'll have the three rooms upstairs. There's only one bathroom I'm afraid, but at least you'll have the floor to yourselves. Charlie and I are downstairs, so you can make yourselves at home."

"You have a lovely house," Maude said, "and it's already decorated for Christmas."

"Mom and I love that sort of thing, so she helped me. Charlie hasn't had time to put the lights up outside, but hopefully he'll do that soon."

Did I hear a hint of annoyance in Cora's voice? I couldn't be sure.

"We got the tree half decorated before Mom realized she had to leave early. If you like you can help me finish it."

"Love to," Maude said.

I smiled politely. Decorating a Christmas tree was not my thing. Kate didn't respond at all, and I wasn't sure she'd even heard the question.

"You must be tired," Cora said. "Get settled upstairs and I'll call you when dinner is ready. Would you like a hot toddy before you head up?"

This time I was the one who was enthusiastic. "If it's not too much trouble," I said, "I'd love one."

"No trouble."

She led us to the kitchen and had us sit at a long farm table.

"Beautiful," Kate said. "Someone made this?"

"Charlie, years ago. You'll find many of the men around here are excellent woodworkers."

"I know," Kate said.

"You know?" Cora asked. "You've been here before?"

"I have."

She said it in such a way that Cora didn't ask any more questions. We watched as Cora put together hot toddies, pouring whiskey, hot water, honey and lemon juice into large glasses. She put a slice of lemon to float on top and a cinnamon stick to stir it all up. "I'd normally give you these before you head off to bed, but they seem just the right thing on this cold afternoon."

"Perfect," I said after a large swallow.

We spent a few minutes visiting and getting the lay of the land.

"You passed by Bob's house on your way here," Cora said. "It's the two-story with the green tin roof. I'll take you there tomorrow. At dinner, we'll talk about what's been happening. For now, simply enjoy your drinks and then get settled upstairs."

That's exactly what we did.

Cora called us to dinner around seven, and we talked about Bob's situation over a delicious meal of oyster stew. "Oysters are what we're known for in Menescotta," Cora said, "so I thought I should start you off right."

Charlie took over most of the conversation. He was much more talkative than he'd been earlier. I guessed he was in his mid-fifties. His hair was beginning to gray and what I imagined had once been a lithesome body was starting to fill out. Cora seemed to feel the need to confess she was older than Charlie, a cougar, she claimed, but she didn't look it. Her brown hair might have come out of a bottle, but you certainly couldn't tell that.

After a good deal of wine, we agreed we'd get to work properly in the morning.

Snow fell softly that night, and I woke early to find the air still and the surroundings a gorgeous white.

I crept downstairs and discovered Cora in the kitchen talking softly. A man I didn't know sat hunched over a mug of coffee. He was wearing dirty overalls, his white beard was wild, and his eyes were bloodshot. This had to be Bob, and once again I wondered if he was a drinking man.

"We didn't expect to see you for hours," Cora said, "but I'm so glad you're up early. This is Bob. And Bob, this is the woman I told you about—Flo Wellington—the one who has the Old Dames Protection Agency."

"ODPA," Bob said. "The agency that keeps people from being murdered. I'm glad to meet you, Ms. Wellington. I hope you can keep me alive until Christmas, but I'm not counting on it."

"Don't say that, Bob." Cora took his hand and squeezed it. "Just tell Ms. Wellington what happened this morning."

She stood and poured me a cup of coffee. "Have a cider doughnut, both of you. They're fresh."

"First of all, call me Flo," I said, "and then let me have two sips of coffee to get myself in gear."

I drank a half cup of coffee and ate most of a doughnut. "There, now I'm ready. What happened to you this morning?"

Bob took a deep breath. He looked at Cora who nodded

at him, and he began. His voice was rough at first, as if he wasn't used to talking—or maybe not talking so early in the morning.

"I usually sleep in during the winter months, maybe until six or seven even. But this morning something woke me, some noise outside. It was five a.m. and still dark of course. It sounded like somebody was breaking into my barn. I got dressed as fast I could. I grabbed Elsie and my dog Patrick and off we went to check things out."

"Elsie?" I asked.

"His rifle," Cora supplied.

"I don't leave home without it," Bob said. "I stepped onto the porch—light was out since yesterday. Put a new bulb in and somebody removed it. That person hadn't figured on a full moon and new snow. I could see plenty. I saw a figure, dressed in black, opening the barn door.

"I shouted at him, but he didn't turn around and he didn't stop. Then I fired a shot into the air. That got his attention. He turned and I saw the glint of a gun. Not a rifle or a shot gun. Something smaller, a revolver, I'd guess.

"Patrick was straining at the leash, barking, growling. But I couldn't let him go—the guy might have shot him—so I closed Patrick back in the house. Then I started running toward the barn. He pointed his gun at me, and I stopped to point my rifle at him.

"Suddenly, something whizzed by the left side of my face. I hit the ground. The figure at the barn seemed as startled as I was. He flung the barn doors open and took off. I watched him run away and got up slowly. My two horses tore out of the barn, scared to death. My old mule sauntered out five minutes later. I looked around. I saw nothing, heard nothing.

"I got the horses and my mule, Hettie, back in the barn. Then I felt something sticky on the side of my face. I was bleeding. That's when I headed over here."

"Turn your head," Cora said, "so Flo can see what happened to you."

Bob turned his head and I could see a wide red line streaking down the left side of his face, from his forehead to his ear. The wound didn't look deep, but its sides looked broad and uneven.

"A shot grazed you?" I asked.

"Must have. I didn't hear a shot. I only felt something whoosh past me. I'm not going to a doctor, so don't start with me about that. Cora will fix me up."

I wasn't about to urge him to get medical attention. The wound looked superficial. "I'm curious about what it was that hit you. You made it sound like it came from behind you, not where your intruder was standing."

"That's how it seemed," Bob said. "The figure I saw was in front of me near the barn doors."

"And the shooter must have been behind you not in front of you for it to graze your face like that."

Bob rubbed his hand along his cheek. "Maybe I turned my head. I don't remember doing that, but I must have."

"Did you hear anything right before it happened—like the cock of a gun?"

Bob was silent. "I heard a jangling, like jingle bells—like bells you might hear on a sleigh."

# 3

I studied Bob. Was he a drinker or was he crazy? The sound of jingle bells, like on a sleigh he didn't see? Next he'd be telling me it was Santa's sleigh on its way to the North Pole. But he hadn't invented the laceration on his face. I'd wait and have Kate take a look at the red line streaking down the left side of his face. She knew more about guns and what they could and couldn't do.

As if on cue, Kate entered the kitchen rubbing her eyes. "Something smells delicious," she said.

Cora handed her a cup of coffee and a doughnut.

"Thank you," Kate said. "Strong coffee and a cider doughnut. Did you make the doughnuts, Cora?"

"I did. I get up early in the winter and end up with time on my hands." Cora pulled out a chair at the farm table. "Here, sit."

I introduced Bob and filled Kate in on what he'd told us. "The bullet, if it was a bullet, apparently brushed his face. Could you take a look at it?"

She glanced at me. I rubbed a hand over my face and tried

to nod slightly with my head in the direction of Bob—anything to give her an indication I thought he might be a little crazy.

"What's wrong with you, Flo?" Kate asked. "Maybe you should go easy on the coffee. You seem to be twitching."

This time I rolled my eyes for the world to see. "Just take a look at the laceration."

"Do you mind if I touch it, Bob?" Kate asked.

Bob shook his head. "Cora's going to fix me up with iodine. An inch closer and she couldn't have fixed up anything about me."

Kate nodded. She ran her hand along the four-inch red line. "You're very lucky. This should heal in a day or two without a scar. Where did you think the shot came from?"

"Don't know. I hit the ground as soon as I heard something whiz past me. Didn't know I was hurt until later."

"You think it came from the intruder by the barn door?" Kate asked.

"The guy with the revolver was opening the barn door—that was my focus. The shot that hit me came out of nowhere. I heard this jingling sound, like from a sleigh, right before it happened. But there wasn't a sleigh, not that I saw."

Kate nodded, as if she believed every word. "That bullet—or whatever it was— traveled down the side of your face from top to bottom."

"You talk like it might not have been a bullet," Bob said. "Why?"

"A lot of things could have caused that cut," Kate said. "I suppose it could have been a bullet, but this is a thick, blurry line. I can't figure out an angle for a shot that would have left a mark like that. It's almost like you scraped against something, Bob. Any chance of that when you were so focused on the barn and it was still dark? Maybe when you fell?"

"Don't know, but I felt something whiz past me."

"You said you fired your gun," I said. "Did the other person fire his revolver?"

"Don't know. Don't think so."

"Do you know if it was a man or woman?" I asked.

"Nope. Dressed all in black, could have been either."

"I assume they were startled to see you there," I said, "and frightened when you fired your rifle."

"They didn't act like it. The person turned so I'd see they had a gun too and they kept fiddling with the barn doors until they could open them."

"The doors were locked?" I asked.

"I don't lock 'em anymore. Had a fire in that barn and nearly lost two horses because the doors were locked, but they do swell when we have a lot of rain or snow. I guess that's why the guy couldn't open them easily. I've always trusted the people around here. Until recently. It's live and let live or it used to be." Bob stood. "I can't worry about this anymore—gotta get back to work."

"I assume you called the police," I said.

"We got a chief of police in Menescotta. He's got four officers, half of them volunteers. They got other things to take care of. What's he gonna do for me?"

"I told Bob he should call them anyway," Cora said. "Let them know there was a prowler on his property. Get it on the record."

"So if I'm found dead one morning, they'll know I wasn't just some crazy old man seeing things in the night." Bob put a hand on Cora's arm as she started to protest. "I know you mean well, Cora, and I'm willing to talk with these women you invited up. But I'm not so keen on talking to the police."

"We'll come round later in the morning," I said. "You'll be home all day?"

"Not going anywhere," he said.

Cora showed him out through the mudroom to the back

door. "Be careful, Bob, those back steps are slippery. Charlie didn't salt them last night even though I asked him to."

This time the annoyance in Cora's voice was unmistakable. Even Bob took note.

"We didn't expect more snow last night, Cora," Bob said. "I didn't salt mine either."

Cora watched Bob clomp down the porch steps in his work boots and waited until he was near his truck before she closed the back door.

"I'll make a proper breakfast when Maude wakes up," she said. "Eggs, bacon, toast—sound good?"

"If you wait for Maude, you'll be fixing us lunch," I said.

Cora laughed. "Then I'll start now and fix her whatever she wants when she gets up."

She went to a basket on a counter top and pulled out half a dozen eggs. "Fresh. You'll love them."

Charlie entered the kitchen a few minutes later. "I caught Bob before he left, and he told me what happened."

Charlie grabbed a cup of coffee and sat, elbows on the table. He leaned forward. It was the first time I noticed the intensity of his blue eyes. Paul Newman blue eyes, I'd have to say.

"I'd love to hear what you make of him," Charlie said to Kate and me. "We've lived next door to Bob for a long time, but we've seen more of him in the last week than we have in the past twenty years. After his wife died, he pretty much shut down. He only pops out for the Santa parade once a year—full of smiles and presents for the kids. Then he's back in his cave. It's not like he's unfriendly. He just doesn't have much to say to anyone unless someone ticks him off. Then he has a lot to say."

"Interesting," I said. "I don't know what to make of his story. It's bizarre."

"I can tell you one thing," Kate said. "It wasn't a bullet that caused that laceration."

"What do you think it was?" I asked.

"It looked a lot like the mark of an arrow, one fired from a height, to make a scratch like that. In the summer before the Olympics I continued to train with folks here—cross-country running and archery. Archery's a completely different sport, but it makes one steady and focused when shooting. Occasionally, an arrow would go astray, and it could leave a mark like that—if it didn't do something much worse."

"So he really did have a scrape with death," I said. "I thought he might be making the whole thing up."

Before we could say more, Maude appeared. She was fully dressed. "A scrape with death? What have I missed?"

Charlie pulled out a chair for Maude and said he needed to check on the animals. "I'll go over to Bob's when I'm done and see if I can find an arrow or whatever might have scratched his face."

Cora asked Maude what she wanted to eat and drink.

"I'm not much of a morning person. Do you have tea?"

"Of course."

We told Maude about our encounter with Bob while Cora made a pot of tea—with loose tea leaves no less. I was falling in love with this woman. She saw me staring at her.

"My mother was Irish," Cora said, "so I know about a good pot of tea. I pretty much make everything from scratch now that I have the time for that."

She must have seen my look. "We're not independently wealthy, Flo, if that's what you're wondering. but our needs are small now that the girls are grown. I work part time as a visiting nurse, and Charlie is a handyman in town. We don't farm much anymore. We keep a few animals and have a vegetable garden during the summer. Charlie's been a little worried about one of the horses—that's why he left, I'm sure."

Cora poured us each a cup of tea as Kate finished her assessment.

"An arrow?" Maude said. "Shot from a height? Like from a rooftop perhaps?"

"Perhaps," Kate said. "Apparently, Bob heard a noise, came out of his house, so depending on where he was standing, the perpetrator could have been on the roof if it were high enough and Bob was close enough."

"Bob has a two-story farm house," Cora said. "He added the second floor when his two kids were teenagers—before his wife died and the kids left home."

Kids? Dead wife? Lots to investigate, I thought.

Never having had kids I was suspicious about what they might get up to. Maybe they hated their father for one reason or another. Maybe one got all the attention and the other was jealous. Maybe one was a bad seed from the start.

Still, hating a jovial Santa was a little hard to believe. That's how Cora and Charlie described Bob at Christmas time, although that certainly wasn't how he seemed this morning. I did a quick calculation. If Bob was mid-sixties, the kids were most likely in their thirties, possibly forties. Wouldn't they have something better to do with their lives than torment their dad or try to kill him?

"Mind telling us where you went just now?" Kate asked.

"I was thinking how kids don't always turn out right. Why did his kids leave home?"

Cora smiled at me. "His kids weren't monsters if that's what you're imagining. They didn't get into drugs although Maine hasn't been spared from the opioid crisis. Someone should go to jail for fostering that, but of course they won't."

"Agreed," the three of us said in unison.

"Anyway, Anise and Albert were good kids," Cora said. "His wife, Ruth, wanted to name them Jack and Jill, but Bob put his foot down."

"Jack and Jill—is that a joke?" I asked.

She laughed. "No joke. Ruth was a kindergarten teacher.

She loved all those nursery rhymes. It could have been worse. Georgie Porgie, Humpty Dumpty, Little Bo Peep."

"The children were twins?" Maude asked.

"Irish twins, born eleven months apart. But they might as well have been the regular kind. They did everything together. Even left home at the same time. They were the world to Bob and Ruth," Cora said, "and then something happened. Some falling out. They left shortly after Ruth died twenty years ago."

"How old are they now?" I asked.

"They'd be in their late thirties."

"Do they live around here?" Maude asked.

Cora shrugged. "I have no idea where they live. Bob never mentions them. He never talks about anything personal. As Charlie said, he hardly talks at all unless he's in his Santa suit. Then he's the most talkative man you'd ever want to meet."

"But he came to you when he thought he was in trouble," Maude said. "He must trust you."

"I think he trusts my husband. Charlie doesn't ask many questions, and they sometimes hunt together. Oh!" she said and stopped talking.

"What?" I asked.

"Bob and Charlie are part of an archery hunting club that started years ago—part of a back-to-nature group. How could I have forgotten that?"

My question exactly. How could she have forgotten that? Unless, she didn't want to put her husband in the cross-hairs so to speak. Was I mixing my metaphors?

Kate gave me a look, a one-eyebrow-raised look that seemed to say she knew what I was thinking and was advising me not to go there. For once I took her unspoken advice.

"Do you know the other members of this club?" I asked. "Is it still active? Did any one of them have a falling out with Bob?"

# 4

We'd finished our tea. I stood up to carry my cup and plate to the large farm house sink. Cora took them out of my hands. "Sit," she said. "I've got this. More tea, Maude, Kate?" she asked.

"Yes, please," Maude said, "if there's more in the pot."

Kate shook her head no. "I'll float away if I have one more cup."

We sat silently waiting for Cora to respond to my question about who was in the hunting club. She poured Maude another cup of tea and gathered up the plates on the table. She took her time rinsing them and then placed them in the dishwasher. Was it my imagination or was she stalling?

She wiped her hands on a towel, brushed her hair back from her face and sat down at the table.

"I don't know much about the club. It's almost like a secret society—like the Masons or something. Sometimes I've felt a little jealous of the hours Charlie spends with the club. According to him, members come and go. You can't become a full-fledged member until you've hunted with the group for a couple of years. Charlie says people get excited about the idea of hunting animals with a bow and arrows. Then, once they discover how difficult it is, they often give up.

"Membership has never gotten much above six or eight folks, I think. So, to answer your question I have no idea who is in the club or what they do at their meetings when they're not hunting. I do know the club almost collapsed a few years back with bad feelings on all sides. Charlie wouldn't tell me any details."

"You seemed reluctant to mention that," I said. "Why?"

"It's nothing really. It's just that Charlie got so upset at the time. I asked what happened, and he wouldn't tell me. It came up suddenly, after a last weekend of hunting."

"When does the hunting season end?" Kate asked.

"The archery season runs from September to December, so it was sometime in late December I think. After it happened, Charlie told me he wasn't sure he'd stay in the club. So many arguments, he said, but that's all he mentioned.

"Do you think he'll talk to us?" Kate asked.

Charlie entered the kitchen with a dozen fresh eggs.

"You can ask him," Cora said taking the basket of eggs from him.

"Ask me what?"

"About the hunting club—the one that's big on bow-and-arrow hunting," I said. "The one that almost disbanded a few years ago over some argument."

"I've never wanted to talk about that. It got ugly fast." He took off his heavy coat and put it over a hook in the mudroom. Then he poured himself a cup of coffee and sat beside Cora.

"I can't see how it could have anything to do with Bob's situation now. It happened at least five years ago."

"At this point we don't know what matters and what doesn't," I said. "We do know someone used a bow and arrow to threaten Bob."

Charlie nodded slowly. "I'll tell you what I remember about

the fight. It was late December, I think. One guy got really upset with the club and with Bob—kind of out of the blue. We'd had our last hunt for the season, but we still met to get ready for the next season. A lot of us made our own arrows, so I think we were working on that. I think it was just after Christmas. Jackson burst in and had it out with Bob."

"Jackson?" I asked.

"Jackson Clark. I knew him as a kid. He was in a Scout troop I led. Always had a temper, and that day he acted as if he were high on something. I never knew why he flew all over Bob. Bob claimed he didn't know either. I worried somebody was going to get hurt. I told Jackson to settle down, and then he turned on me. The other guys restrained him. Bob got in his face and told him to stop acting like a damn fool. Jackson left at that point, but he said he'd be back.

"I could see he was upset, so I tried to find him later. He'd left town, and I never saw him again. Bob called him a troublemaker and said it was a good thing he was gone."

"For a quiet man," I said, "Bob seems to get himself in the middle of a lot of turmoil."

"I hadn't thought about it before," Charlie said, "but you're right, he does. He has a bad temper too. I guess he and I never argue because I never press him on things. We can be together for hours, fishing, hunting, and say four words to each other."

"Bob's a rigid man," Cora said. "Wouldn't you describe him that way, Charlie? He likes things done exactly right—what he thinks is right. If I offered him tea, he'd make sure I steeped it for precisely five minutes."

Charlie nodded. "Yep, that's Bob. We store our gear in a shed Bob has behind his house. He notices when things aren't the way he left them—lined up in a neat row, snapped into their spots on the back of the wall. If anything is out of order he throws a fit. Two weeks ago he said some of his arrows were missing. He was furious. He said no one was supposed to touch his gear. He confronted the folks in the club. A couple of men left at that point. They said they'd had enough of the club and of Bob."

"Do you have the names of people in the club?" I asked. "Could you give us a list?"

Charlie stood and poured himself another cup of coffee. He remained standing near the sink.

"You think one of those guys is threatening Bob?" Charlie asked. "I've known a lot of those guys my whole life." He shook his head. "I don't know about a list. Up here, we don't meddle in other people's business. No offense, Flo."

"None taken," I said, "but Cora's mother invited us up here to keep Bob safe, and we need to know who might bear a grudge against him—maybe someone who knows how to use a bow and arrow. She's worried about Bob's safety. Aren't you?"

Charlie took off his cap and scratched his blond head now graying at the temples. "Sure I am, but the idea that one of our hunting buddies might try to hurt Bob—that I can't buy."

"And the guy who left the club?" I asked. "Jackson somebody?"

"Jackson Clark. He's been gone five years."

"Will you give us the other names?"

"I'm not ready to give out names of people who couldn't have anything to do with what's going on now," Charlie said. It was the first time I saw his affable facade slip a little.

"Charlie," Cora said. "This isn't about loyalty to your old boys' club. This is about Bob's safety."

"You've never appreciated that club," Charlie said. He sounded angry. "You seem to think it took something away from us, Cora. It didn't do that."

"Someone shot an arrow at Bob," Kate said. "They were either a very good shot in the middle of the night, or it was a lucky accident Bob wasn't killed."

Charlie put his cap back on.

"All right," he said. "I'll give you the list, but I need to tell the guys first you'll be coming round. If not, they'll cut me off."

"That sounds fair," Maude said.

"Did you find an arrow?" I asked.

"I didn't make it to Bob's yet. I thought you might want the eggs first. I'll head over now."

He grabbed his heavy coat from the mudroom and pulled it on. Then he poked his head back into the kitchen. "It's a funny thing. Whoever is doing this knows exactly how to get Bob where it hurts. First, his Santa costume—he's as fastidious about that as he is about everything else. Then his horses. That's the one time Bob and I might have a long discussion—we both love our horses. We used to take long rides together. You remember that, Cora?"

"Of course. When Ruth was alive, the four of us would ride for hours."

"So, if someone was going to do something to one of his horses, Bob might go berserk," Charlie said. "I'd worry more about that fellow's safety than Bob's."

"How did his wife die and when?' I asked.

"Twenty years ago," Charlie said. "Fell off a mountain top when she was hiking. Alone. She was an experienced hiker and walked that path often. Some people in town wondered if it was really an accident."

# 5

Kate told me to close my mouth. I admit I was stunned. An experienced hiker is killed when she falls off a mountain top. I'm sure it happens from time to time, but it wasn't as if Ruth had been climbing Mount Everest.

"Was it bad weather or a tricky path?" I asked.

"Nope," Charlie said. "It was a sunny morning when she fell."

"Did anyone see her fall?" Kate asked.

"Nope," Charlie said again. "It was a hike she took all the time. Sometimes you went with her, didn't you, Cora?"

"Yes, often. I wished I'd done it that day."

The words came out slowly, and it felt as if Cora might be reliving that horrible day. She got up from the table and stood staring out the window at the white landscape, the bare trees glistening from last night's snow. I could see the trees from where I sat, but I had the feeling they weren't what Cora was seeing.

"I think we all have regrets about that day," she said. "If

only one of us had been there, we could have prevented a tragedy that feels as if it happened yesterday."

"Do either of you know any more about what happened?" I asked.

They both shook their heads.

"Bob wouldn't talk to me about it," Charlie said.

"He wouldn't say much to me either," Cora said, "but I could see how distraught he was. I'd bring him dinner almost every night. When I couldn't do it friends from the care committee at church took over. He was so sad. It seemed as if he'd lost his will to live. He told me how concerned he was about the children, especially Anise. What did he know about raising a teenage girl on his own? Anise was fifteen and seemed to be as lost as he was."

"And Albert?" I asked.

"Albert was sixteen," Cora said. "He'd always been rebellious, but after his mother died, he got worse. He wouldn't listen to a thing Bob said. Then Bob found a woman to help with the children. He seemed to feel a great weight had been lifted off his shoulders. She wasn't local, so I didn't know much about her. She was a lot younger than Bob."

"A good-looking woman," Charlie said.

Cora gave him a look. "Charlie notices these things."

"It's like I notice a pretty sunset or a neighbor's apple tree. Doesn't mean I'm going to steal the fruit."

"I know." She patted his arm. "At least I think I know."

This sounded like an old discussion, and one I wasn't about to get into.

"Did the kids like her?" I asked. "Did she stick around?"

"She did more than stick around," Cora said. "After three months she and Bob were engaged. Then a few weeks after their engagement was announced everything fell apart. You asked if the kids liked her—I don't think so. Not from what our daughter Julie said. She was friends with Anise. According to

Julie, the woman didn't take care of Anise or Albert—not that either one wanted her to do that. But they didn't want to be sent away to a boarding school either, and that seemed to be what she was pushing Bob to do."

"Do you remember the name of the woman?" Kate asked.

"Betty?" Cora said, looking at Charlie.

"No. Beatrice. Beatrice Lohman," he supplied.

"I guess you did take an interest," Cora said.

"I'd have to say all the men in town took an interest in her. She was a standout in our little town. She always dressed to show off her best assets, and she had plenty of those. Some people thought she must be an actress or a model—the way she held herself. And if a camera was anywhere near by, she smiled as if she were about to appear on the cover of some fancy magazine."

"The women in the town," Cora said, "were more concerned about the welfare of the children and Bob."

"We cared about Bob's welfare," Charlie said. "Frankly, we couldn't imagine what she saw in him or why she'd want to live in a small town like Menescotta. Two thousand people—what would a beautiful woman want in a town like that? You could tell she was sophisticated. Not snooty, I wouldn't say that—just big city sophisticated—like maybe she came from Portland."

The big city of Portland, I thought, but didn't say.

"Bob's daughter, Anise, was convinced the attraction was all about money," Cora said.

"Bob was a wealthy man?" I asked.

"Was and is," Cora said. "He doesn't flaunt it, but he owns a lot of farmland west of Menescotta. He'll never sell it. I always wondered if that's what caused that woman to leave town finally."

"*That* woman?" Maude asked. "You didn't like her, Cora?"

Cora paused. "I guess I didn't. She was never rude to me, more like a cold fish. I couldn't imagine what Bob saw in her."

"I could," Charlie said and chuckled.

Cora ignored him. "She was the opposite of Ruth. Ruth loved living here. If anyone needed anything, Ruth was on the spot to provide it. Not Beatrice. I never saw her give a helping hand to anyone."

"How long was she here?" I asked.

"Less than a year," Cora said.

"She certainly made a strong impression on people in a short amount of time," Maude said.

"She did," Cora said with a sidelong glance at Charlie.

"How did Bob take her leaving?" Maude asked.

"You know, I thought he'd be crushed," Cora said, "but I think he was relieved."

"Do you think maybe he's the one who broke it off?" I asked.

"That's not the story he told me," Cora said. "He said Beatrice decided she couldn't live in a small town, and he knew he wasn't going to leave Menescotta."

"That's the story we heard, too," Charlie said.

"We?" I asked.

"The boys in the hunting club," Charlie said. "It was a regular hunting club until someone got the bright idea of making it a bow-and-arrow hunting club—that was a few years after Ruth died."

"Anise and Albert left before Beatrice did," Cora said.

"Do you know why?" Maude asked.

"No," she said.

"Where did they go?" I asked.

"Ruth had a sister in upstate Maine, near the Canadian border. I think they went there to live and then onto college in Canada."

"Do they come back to visit?" Maude asked.

"Anise comes back sometimes, always at Christmas," Cora said. "I think that's one reason Bob loves the holidays and playing Santa. That's what really brought him out of his depression, don't you think, Charlie? Our old Santa had died and Bob took over the role, what— fifteen years ago? He had the right body for it and it wasn't hard for him to grow a beard. At first he had to dye it white, but now it looks just the way it should. In that costume, Bob seemed to come out of himself. It was amazing to see!"

"It was," Charlie said. "He started playing Santa five years after Ruth died and never missed a season. The town is buying him a new costume, but I'm not sure he's up for it this year."

"Is he frightened about what someone might do?" I asked.

"Not frightened so much," Cora said, "more discouraged. He told me, 'If people don't want me around, I won't force myself on anyone.' "

Charlie stood and Cora followed. "I'm really sorry, but we have to go into town," she said. "I have a shut-in to visit, and Charlie has supplies to buy. We'll stop by Bob's on the way. Make yourself at home—we should be back by noon, in time for lunch."

We watched them leave through the back door and climb into Charlie's truck.

Maude made another pot of tea. Kate and I looked at each other—it was likely Maude would be drinking this pot on her own.

"Their timing is perfect," I said. "Now we can start to figure out what's really going on—laptop, Kate?"

"Upstairs, back in a minute."

I sat and watched Maude pour hot water over the tea leaves and set the stove timer for five minutes.

"In every British mystery I've ever seen," Maude said, "the detectives always have a cup of tea to help them think."

"I'll do better with another cider doughnut," I said.

Maude handed me one.

So many possible suspects, such a joy for someone like me.

Beatrice, Albert, Anise, members of the hunting club. I wondered who suggested they take on bow-and-arrow hunting —probably someone skilled at that. And according to Kate, whoever shot the arrow that scraped Bob's face was either an excellent archer or a very bad one. Of course, another possibility was that Bob was leading us on a wild goose chase— either deliberately or because he'd gone around the bend. Could he have created the laceration along the side of his face? I'd have to ask Kate about that.

She returned with her laptop. Maude poured herself a cup of tea, and I finished off the doughnut. Then we settled in to do some work.

# 6

Maude took a sip of tea and smiled. "If I lived in England I could have a cuppa whenever I wanted one and have high tea in the afternoon. Sometimes I think I should move there."

"Maybe later," I said. "We need you here right now."

I always got a little nervous when people talked about leaving. Maude and I were a well-oiled machine. We were a team—like Rogers and Hammerstein, Holmes and Watson, Bonnie and Clyde. Well, maybe not Bonnie and Clyde. To be honest, it was her friendship I'd miss terribly if she ever did decide to leave.

"We can have high tea whenever you want it, Maude," I said, "Marianne won't mind fixing it for us."

Maude patted my hand. "I'm not really going anywhere, Flo. No worries. Where shall we start?" she asked.

"I'd like to start with the hunting club," I said. "From what you said, Kate, it had to be a very skillful archer to cause that laceration on the side of Bob's face. Or it was dumb luck."

"I'd vote for skill," Kate said. "If the arrow was meant to kill Bob, it would have been easily done. Aim for his torso.

Stand directly in front or behind him, but not from a great height. No, I think it's pretty clear, someone wanted to toy with him for a while before they finished the job."

"If they even want to finish the job," I said. "It might be they want to push him over the edge, and they seem to be doing a good job of that. Is there any chance Bob could be behind his misadventures—maybe to get attention?"

"Why would you say that?" Maude asked. "I like Bob, and he's been through so much."

"No offense, Maude, but you like everyone," I said. "If we relied on your initial impressions, we'd never catch a murderer —not before they committed the act, anyway." I turned to Kate. "Any chance Bob could have created that laceration himself and then made it look like the scrape of an arrow?"

"Possible," Kate said. "I suppose a sharpened stick could do it—but it would have been painful. And what would be his motive? He seems to be a man who doesn't like attention."

"You have a point," I said, "unless he really is whacko."

"Let's table that idea for now," Kate said.

She started clicking away on her laptop. "I thought I'd see if this Menescotta bow-and- arrow club has gotten any notice." She paused for a moment and seemed to be reading something. Then she scrolled down and punched a few more keys. "I can't believe this! You know who was a member of this hunting club?"

She didn't wait for a response. She pushed her laptop in my direction.

In front of me was a picture of a young woman in her twenties, I'd guess, in full archery regalia with a name below her picture—Fiona Dickerson—and an article that said she was destined to be Maine's great hope in the coming Olympics. I looked at the date—it was from five years ago.

"Fiona Dickerson?" I asked. "Should that name mean something to me?"

"She's only the best archer that's ever lived in Maine, maybe in the country," Kate said, "maybe in the world."

"I love the Olympics," Maude said, "but I've never heard of her."

"That's because she had to drop out," Kate said. "Rumors from my archery buddies here in Maine said it was because she was pregnant. I wonder if Cora and Charlie would know the real story."

"So she was in the archery hunting club five years ago?" I asked.

"She was its most famous member, obviously," Kate said.

"That's interesting," I said, "but that was five years ago."

Kate took back her laptop. "There's more. The latest edition of the Menescotta Gazette says she's back in town to be with her father. It says he's ailing."

Kate smiled. It was the first real smile I'd seen from her in a while. "I'd love to meet her and here she is in town." Then she stopped smiling. "If she's caring for an ailing father, I can't intrude on that."

"Unless she's a suspect or might give us valuable information," I said.

"Yes!" Kate said and then she frowned. "I won't be happy if she's a suspect. What could she possibly have against Bob? On the other hand, she might know a lot about the other members of this club."

"Does it mention the other club members by name?" I asked.

"No. It only talks about her," Kate said.

"All right, then," I said. "Moving on. Let's see what you find out about Beatrice Lohman? She sounds the sort who might want revenge—if Bob really was the one who called it off."

"After twenty years?" Maude asked.

"You know that saying," I said, " 'Revenge is a dish best served cold.' "

"After twenty years," Maude said, "the food wouldn't be cold it would be rotten with maggots all over the plate."

"Maude, you made a joke!" I said. "I've never heard you make a joke before."

"I'm not sure I meant to make one," she said. "Don't you think Beatrice Lohman would have taken her revenge immediately—breach of promise perhaps. And as to Fiona Dickerson as a possible suspect? Kate seems to think the world of this woman, so I have trouble believing she's a bad person."

"You always see the best in people," I said.

"And you tend to imagine the worst, Flo," Maude said.

"I'm just saying no one, not even this Fiona Dickerson, can be above suspicion. She needs to go on our list."

I looked over at Kate for a little help. Kate based her opinion on the facts.

She made a face. "We'll put her on the list and then see what Cora and Charlie know about her. She's a fantastic archer and could easily have spun that arrow next to Bob's face, and she's back in town. But why would she do that? I'd prefer to think of her as a material witness. She'd know the other guys who might be handy with a bow and arrow, and that way I'll have an excuse to meet her!"

I didn't want to rain on Kate's parade. It was the first time in weeks I'd seen her so animated.

"Okay," I said. "Moving on."

I stood and stretched. I walked to the window above the large farm sink and looked out at the snow-covered yard. It was hard to imagine mayhem when the outside world looked so serene. In the distance I could see snow-topped hills. On the drive from Portland to Menescotta, we'd passed rocky cliffs as if the road had been gouged through them. If Ruth had fallen onto rocks like those, she'd never have survived.

The soft tolling of a church bell brought me back to the present, and I sat down again.

"Let's get back to business," I said. "We can't do anything about the hunting club for the moment, but let's see what we can find out about Beatrice Lohman. I wish we had a date of birth."

"Let me tackle this," Kate said. She started typing furiously on her laptop.

Pause.

`More furious typing. "I've found a dozen Beatrice Lohmans listed in the US. I'm guessing she'd be at least fifty by now, thirty or so when she stayed with Bob. Here are some photos."

She turned her laptop toward Maude and me.

"She'd be good-looking," Maude said. "That's what Charlie said."

"Twenty years ago," I added. "How about this one?"

Kate swung the laptop back to her and typed. "No go. Happily married to Mr. Lohman for thirty years, high school sweethearts, three grown kids. They live in California."

We went through three more Beatrice Lohmans before giving up.

"We don't even know if that's her current name," Kate said. "Maybe she married once she left Bob."

"Okay," I said. "We'll table that for now. Bob might give us more information if he's willing to talk to us. That's where you come in, Maude. You can get anyone to talk."

"Shall we try to track the kids?" Kate asked. "They have names we might find and no reason to change them."

"Yes, let's track the kids," I said.

"Anise Quellette," Kate said. "Here we go. Now, Anise Hall. Living in upstate Maine with a new husband—a potato farmer. She must be the one—here's her picture."

Maude and I studied it.

"How many people in Maine have the name Anise?" Maude asked.

"She's the one," I said. "Look at her eyes, her round face." We were studying a wedding photo. "Can you get a close-up?"

"Here you go," Kate said.

I had to admit if I were a person who gave out compliments, I'd be showering Kate with praise.

"Yes, that's Anise," I said. "Her round face, her eyes look just like Bob's. So, I suspect she's off our list. Why would a newly married woman decide to torment her father no matter how unhappy she might have been with him in the past? Unless she's after his money. From what I've heard, potato farming is a hard life and not always profitable."

"You are so cynical," Kate said.

"Realistic, I prefer to say."

"Whatever," Kate said, "we take her off the suspect list."

"Agreed," Maude said.

"You're probably right," I said, "but for now, let's put her on the bottom of the list. On to Albert."

Before we could move on to Albert, Cora and Charlie burst through the back door and into the kitchen.

"You won't believe what just happened!" Cora said.

# 7

Cora and Charlie took off their scarves and hats, but they didn't bother to remove anything else.

"Please tell me Bob is still alive," I said.

"Better than alive," Cora said. "We thought we should stop by and see him on our way to town. He said he'd changed his mind about everything—he no longer felt his life was in danger. He's going to be in the parade, give out the gifts to the kids as he's done for the last fifteen years. He was actually smiling."

Cora was smiling too. She removed her coat and boots, put them in the mudroom and returned in her house slippers. Charlie stayed put.

"What happened?" I asked.

"Bob said he'd had an epiphany of some kind," Charlie said. "He realized if someone was actually threatening his life he'd be dead by now. He called himself an easy target. He decided that whoever was doing this might be trying to spoil Christmas for the kids in Menescotta, and he wasn't going to let that happen."

"What?" I said. "You don't actually believe that nonsense, do you?"

That seemed to catch both of them off guard. "Actually, we do," Cora said after a few seconds. "Maybe you don't know what a big deal Santa is in Menescotta. People come from miles around—from Portland, from Augusta, everywhere. It all starts in a few days. First, Santa arrives in a boat on the river. Then he rides down Main Street in his sleigh. After that, every family in Menescotta with kids invites Santa for a visit until the 24th. Once a week a dinner is held at the town hall. You'll be here for most of it. You'll see what a big deal it is."

"So," Maude said slowly, "what about the shredded Santa clothes, the arrow that could have killed Bob?"

Charlie spoke before Cora could. "Bob said he never found an arrow, and if there was one it wasn't meant to kill him. He didn't exactly call it divine intervention, more like it wasn't his time yet."

"He's had a complete transformation," I said. "Someone must have reassured him, someone he trusts. That's the only reasonable explanation. Maybe Bob's right, but he could be dead wrong, and I won't let that happen on my watch."

"You think someone would harm him in front of the kids?" Cora asked. "No one in Menescotta would do that, no matter what axe they had to grind with Bob personally."

"Bad choice of words," I said. "Maybe they wouldn't do it in front of the kids. The two earlier attacks were done at Bob's house. In any case, we need to see who's behind this mischief."

"Agreed," Kate said.

"We'll head over to Bob's," I said. "A brisk morning walk will do us all good."

Kate stood and nodded. She tucked her laptop into its case and grabbed her coat. Maude and I did the same.

"You can't walk from here," Charlie said. "The temperature's dropping, and it could be icy. I'll drive you. Besides, I still have errands to run in town, so I'll head there next."

We piled into Charlie's roomy truck, complete with a back seat. It was a short ride over beautiful countryside—fresh snow everywhere. We were at Bob's house in minutes.

"Visitors," Charlie yelled as he approached the door. "You decent?"

Bob opened the door before we knocked. "I'm always decent." He greeted us looking like a new man. He was wearing clean overalls and his beard was neatly trimmed. "Come on in."

"I've got business in town," Charlie said. "Call me when you need a ride back."

"I'll take 'em," Bob said. "Need to make sure my sleigh is working all right. I'll hitch up Addy and Bessie."

"Your horses?" Maude asked, "the ones the person with the gun wanted to steal?"

"I think I got that wrong. I'd had a little too much to drink, and I think I got things mixed up. I think maybe I forgot to close the barn door, and then in the wind I thought someone was out there opening it."

"And the scrape on your cheek?" Kate asked, examining it once more. "You made that up as well? Not an arrow or a gun—just your imagination."

"Now you're putting me on, Miss Kate. I didn't imagine that, but I'll bet you I stumbled and thought I heard something. A confused old man. I'm better now, a lot better."

"I think we should talk about why you're so much better, Bob," I said. "Maybe we could do that inside—by a fire if you have one."

"Sure, sure. Sorry. I feel so good I forgot you were standing out here in the cold. Come in."

I started to wonder if Bob had taken something to make him feel so good. He led us into the parlor, started a fire and helped us out of our coats. I felt as if we were in a time warp. The parlor looked exactly the way it probably looked one hundred and fifty years ago. There were gas lamps on two of the tables and a gas chandelier overhead. On the arms and back of what felt like a horsehair sofa were antimacassars. The sofa itself was a brilliant red with elaborate wooden carving across the top.

Bob must have seen me fidgeting. "Try this chair instead, Flo. It's not horsehair. Ruth allowed me to buy it shortly before she died."

"Thanks, Bob. I love the rosewood even if the sofa is not terribly comfortable."

"Ruth cared about history," Bob said. "This was an old farm house when we bought it—built in the 1800s. Ruth said at least one room should be preserved in the style of the time. She insisted on an elegant style, and this is it."

"It's beautiful," Maude said. "You must think about her every time you come in here."

"Not everyone realizes that," Bob said. "I don't mean to pry, but did you lose someone dear to you?"

"A daughter. I see her in my granddaughter."

"Hmm, yes," he said. "I see Ruth in Anise."

"We heard both your children were living away from here," Maude said gently. "You make it sound as if you've seen Anise recently."

"Went to her wedding," Bob said, "last month. She didn't want me to walk her down the aisle, but she said I could come. That's all I wanted. I thought we were good and then my son came and caused a fuss, and Anise ended up sending me off."

"It was after the wedding that your troubles started," I said. "Any connection between those events?"

"You mean did my son or daughter want to cause me trouble? I don't believe that."

"Why did your son make a fuss?" Maude asked.

"He always makes a fuss. He's never believed my side of the story."

"What story and what side?" I asked.

"I don't want to go there. Everything's fine now. I'm sorry Cora dragged you up here— wasted trip."

"I hope you're right, Bob," I said. "But your quick turn-around makes me nervous. Who convinced you that you had nothing to worry about?"

"That's private. I promised I wouldn't tell anyone what I was told, and I won't break my word. Just take it from me, all my problems are over. Now, can I give you girls a sleigh ride? You stay here while I get the horses ready."

He left us warming ourselves by the fire.

Two minutes later, Bob ran back into the house.

"Got to call Doc Meadows—the vet. Bessie's gone and Addy's got an arrow in her side."

# 8

"You girls stay put," Bob said. "I got to see to my horse."

"Do you need help?" Kate asked.

"Charlie's on his way. We can handle it."

We watched Bob leave by the front door. He pounded down the steps and got his truck backed up close to a horse trailer. Charlie arrived as Bob got the trailer hooked up. Together they coaxed Addy out of the barn. From where we were I couldn't see if Addy still had an arrow in her side.

"She's moving well," Kate said. "Looks skittish, but I can't see she's in pain."

"Can you see an arrow sticking out from that poor horse?" Maude asked.

"No. They must have removed it," Kate said. "It'd be too dangerous to ride to the vet's office with that arrow still in her. She's up and not limping—that's a good sign. If she were really in trouble, they would have had the vet come to them."

We waved at them from the open front door as they drove past. Charlie waved back, and Bob yelled, "Close that door—you gals will freeze, and I don't want that on my conscience."

We shut the door, and it was only then I noticed we were all shivering. "To the fire," I said and led the way back to the parlor.

"I guess the danger isn't past," Maude said rubbing her hands in front of the remaining embers. "Should we look for the other horse, Bessie?"

"Where would we start?" I asked. "Bob told us to stay put, and I think that's good advice."

"As in stay in this parlor?" Maude asked.

"Seems to me we have free rein of the house," I said. "Let's make use of it."

"I don't think Bob meant for us to snoop through his house," Kate said. She'd already put another log in the fire and was bringing it back to life.

"He didn't tell us not to," I said, "and besides, Bob is completely unaware of what he needs. He thinks everything's fine because someone told him it was fine. And now one horse has disappeared and another is wounded." I stood. "Come on. We have no idea how far away the vet is or how long he'll be gone. Let's go. Divide and conquer. Maude, you stay on the first floor. I'll handle the second. Kate, you look for what might be useful—a cell phone, a computer, whatever. We'll meet back here in half an hour."

Off we went. The second floor contained three bedrooms and two bathrooms. Two of the bedrooms looked out on the front yard. The third, which was larger than the others, looked out the back. Bob might be a wealthy landowner, but you couldn't tell that from his house. Everything was clean but dated—from the wallpaper to the mustard-colored bathroom that stood between the two bedrooms at the front of the house. I doubted that he'd made any changes to the decor since his wife died.

The only thing that looked upgraded—and by upgraded I mean new within the last twenty years—was the ensuite bathroom to the master bedroom. Maybe that was something the interloper Beatrice Lohman insisted upon before their engagement fell apart. It was a neutral white and contained two sinks, plenty of storage space, along with a bath and shower.

I'd start there. Sometimes the oddest things were tucked away in bathrooms. I went through the drawers. Most were empty. One contained make-up. If Bob was so fastidious, why hadn't he thrown that out, and who did it belong to? I couldn't imagine his keeping anything of Beatrice's around, unless he secretly hoped she'd return to him.

I examined it. No expensive brands. More importantly, it wasn't old. Not twenty years old, anyway. Mascara, lipstick, blush. This was make-up a young woman might use, not someone older who would need a lot more than those three items to look respectable.

I studied my own face in the mirror. Goodness. I needed to see my cosmetologist. Why hadn't she offered me a new wrinkle cream?

Maybe it was bad lighting.

Ah, well, back to business. If in fact this was the make-up of a young woman, we had only one of those on our list who was likely to be staying in Bob's house—his daughter, Anise. Had she been the one who'd come to visit and assured Bob that all was well? Hmm. I could spin a story—that she'd talked to her brother, that she'd convinced him to stay away from their dad.

But what was the issue between Albert and Bob? Had the danger really been resolved so easily? I looked for other signs that Anise might have been in the house recently. I checked the trash can for hair and searched for a hairbrush but found nothing.

I went back into the master bedroom. The bed was neatly made. Everything about the room was neat, almost as if no one slept there. I looked in the drawers of the nearest bedside table. One turned down picture in the top drawer showed the four of them together—Bob, thirty years younger with no beard, a person I assumed to be Ruth, kind face and open smile, and the two young children, Albert and Anise. It was a studio portrait. At the bottom of the picture was the inscription: "Merry Christmas, Bob. All our love, always." The children looked to be five and six. Albert was holding on to his mother's hand, and Anise was standing close to Bob. A warm family photograph.

Why didn't Bob have that picture out where it belonged? Couldn't he bear to look at it? But if that was the case, why hadn't he stashed it away in the attic or someplace else? Every time he opened the drawer he'd see the picture, whether or not he allowed himself to look at it.

There were three drawers in each bedside table, and I searched them carefully. I found a Bible in the second drawer and a smattering of papers in the third. This might take time. I hadn't hit a gold mine of lost love letters, but the papers weren't trash either. I sorted through them carefully and placed them in piles. One pile seemed to be a collection of newsletters from the agricultural society of Menescotta, which discussed the latest farming suggestions. These seemed to focus on berries in the summer season and apples in the fall. A second pile contained church announcements—the ones you'd pick up when you attended a service. Why would he keep those? I checked dates. The latest one was from twenty years ago.

Each contained a mention of Bob's family. One included Ruth on a prayer list. One noted communion classes that both Anise and Albert attended. It appeared Bob was Lutheran. Another announcement noted the engagement between him and Beatrice Lohman. The wedding was planned for the new year—twenty years past—and everyone was invited.

The final piece of paper in what I was calling the religious file was the obituary for Ruth Quellette, "beloved wife of

Robert Quellette, survived by Robert and their two children Anise and Albert."

I checked my watch. I'd spent fifteen minutes in this room and hadn't seen the rest of the bedrooms. I skimmed the rest of the obituary. It didn't mention cause of death. I put back the papers and attempted to scatter them the way Bob had.

Then I sorted through the drawers in the other bedside table. Nothing but books, lots of books. Most of them appeared to be romance novels—not exactly what I imagined Bob would be reading. More evidence someone younger and female had been staying in this room.

I turned back the quilt and found what I was looking for—a strand of long blond hair on a pillow. Someone had recently stayed over, someone like Anise.

I didn't have time for a thorough search of the other bedrooms. I did what I could with my last fifteen minutes. If we had time, we'd come up and do a better search. The bedroom across the hall seemed to be where Bob was staying. His clothes were in the drawers, his boots in the closet, and pajamas were hanging on a hook. In the rear of the closet was a large plastic box labeled Santa costume. I took off the lid and found a carefully folded, completely intact Santa outfit. His new one? I didn't think the town had finished that for him yet.

Had Bob made up the story of the slashed costume? Could anyone verify that it had been shredded and his boots covered with paint? Surely, they would have looked. Ida would have looked at it before she asked for our help, wouldn't she?

I yelled downstairs about what I'd found and heard Kate's voice in return.

"Come quick. You have to see this!"

# 9

I ran downstairs. To be honest, at my age, I don't run anywhere. Not that I ever did. It's completely undignified. However, in this instance, I grabbed the handrail and moved quickly. Maude and Kate met me at the bottom of the stairs. Kate held a paper in her hands. It was a quitclaim deed. I'd seen one before—a friend of my father's used it to sign over property to a relative.

Kate pointed out the pertinent details. "Bob signed over his property to his daughter, Anise, yesterday. Look at the date!"

"And today Bob suddenly feels his worries are over," I said.

"Exactly," Kate said.

We didn't have time to say more. We heard someone driving up Bob's snow-covered driveway.

Kate grabbed the paper out of my hands and dashed into the kitchen. I followed her in time to see her stuff the deed into a giant coffee can and place it back on a shelf.

"Interesting safe," I said.

"His valuables seem to be hidden all over this kitchen," Maude said. "We found money, jewelry and ribbons that said

'Best in Show' for one of his horses from a summer agrarian fair."

As Maude was talking, she poured water into three mugs and plopped a tea bag in each. "I always bring an emergency supply of tea bags," she said. "Pretend it's hot."

"We're in the kitchen," Kate yelled when she heard someone entering the front door.

Bob and Charlie appeared at the kitchen door as we sipped our very disgusting cups of cold tea.

"We made ourselves at home," I said. "I hope you don't mind."

"I don't mind," Bob said, "now that I know Addy's okay. The doc says the wound is superficial. He wants to keep her for a day or two to make sure it heals properly, but he says there's nothing to worry about. He said she shouldn't pull the sleigh this year in the parade. The halter will rub against the wound, so that's a problem. Bessie is old, and I haven't had her pull the sleigh for years."

"Any sign of Bessie?" Maude asked.

"No, but I'm not too worried about her," Bob said. "She's wandered off before. She'll be back."

Bob seemed remarkably calm for a man who loved his horses.

"Are you still convinced your problems are over?" I asked. "Someone seems to be after your horses even if they've given up trying to harm you—which I also doubt."

Bob sat down at the table and ran a hand along the laceration on the left side of his face. It already looked much better.

"Do you have more hot water?" Bob asked. "I could use a cup of tea."

"Sorry, no," Maude said. "Wouldn't you rather have coffee?"

She looked around, and I realized all she saw was the

coffee tin containing the quitclaim deed. I jumped up and grabbed the can.

Charlie reached out to stop me. He pointed to a can beside the coffee maker. "Coffee's in there."

But I already had the can open. Bob didn't seem fazed by the situation. He sat rubbing his cheek and staring at me.

"How curious," I said innocently, "what in the world is this?"

I unrolled the paper we'd carefully stashed back in the tin. I pretended to examine it. "It says it's a quitclaim deed. How odd. Signed yesterday."

Kate stood beside me. "It says your property has been signed over to Anise. Is that your signature?"

Bob waved the paper away. "Sure it is."

If anyone looked upset, it was Charlie. "You promised you'd give me first crack at buying your land when you were ready to sell. You told me you even put that in your will. You know I'd give you a good offer."

"You'll still have a crack at it. You'll just deal with my daughter and her new husband, that's all. It's likely they'll want to sell some of the land if not all of it. No need to get upset, Charlie." Bob shrugged. "I didn't mean for any of this to come to light, but I'm glad it has."

"Would you mind filling us in on what's going on?" I asked.

"Don't mind a bit," Bob said and smiled. "I want this out in the open. Whoever thinks they can threaten me will stop now. I figure someone wanted to drive me off my land, make me sell. If they actually wanted to kill me I'd be dead. Now, the problem is solved. I don't own this land anymore. No one has to force me out of Menescotta—they can leave me in peace."

"What makes you think that, Bob?" Maude asked.

"It's a long story. Better make us a big pot of coffee, Maude. Use the tin Charlie's holding."

Maude got to work.

"You know," Bob said warmly. as he watched her work, "you look a lot like my Ruth—doing what needs doing. Same warm smile."

Maude blushed, and I began to wonder if Bob had designs on Maude despite the obvious and enormous age difference. There was a name for a man who was the male version of a cougar—a man interested in an older woman—a manther, but it didn't have nearly the same ring to it. I guess it didn't happen much.

"The story?" I reminded him.

"Settle in," Bob said. "You too, Charlie. I'm sorry I didn't tell you first. I didn't expect any of this to go public just yet. A lot of folks have been bugging me to sell property I had no intention of selling."

"Like who?" Charlie asked.

"Like Rudolph Samson, for one."

"Doesn't he have all the money and land he could possibly want?" Charlie asked.

"Should have, but for folks like him, nothing is ever enough. You know that, Charlie. He's been ticked at me ever since I got that petition signed and worked to keep him from being elected Selectman in November. He thought he was invincible and couldn't stand it when he found he wasn't."

I looked at Kate. I'm sure my expression said it all. A suspect in capital letters. She took out a note pad and jotted down the name.

"We need to hear a lot more about this Rudolph Samson," I said. "What petition and why hasn't anyone mention him before?"

"Because he's a blowhard," Bob said, "that's why. I can't stand the man, and most of Menescotta agrees with me. I got a petition signed against him when he was trying to bring in a

Walmart to Menescotta—on land he just happened to own. We don't want that here, some big box store to ruin our land, drag in people from everywhere. I got 2500 people to sign that petition. That's more people than live in Menescotta. That got the Selectmen's attention, I can tell you." Bob chuckled. "He wanted to be a Selectman—thought he'd have more influence that way. He lost to a woman this past November. Pure humiliation for Samson. He's nothing."

"Maybe so," I said, "but if you humiliated him the way you say you did and kept him from making a financial killing with a sale of land to Walmart, he must be very angry, and he might be out for revenge."

"Possible, but I don't see that," Bob said. "He's a coward."

Bob smiled as Maude poured him a cup of coffee. "What else did you find when you girls rummaged through my house?"

We all tried to look shocked at his accusation, and we all failed miserably. I know I did.

"You don't think I know what you've been up to—grabbing the can the way you did. The Old Dames Protection Agency. Detectives. What would a detective do but rummage through the house of a suspect when the coast was clear?"

"A suspect?" I asked.

"Flo, I've seen the way you look at me, as if I might be making up the whole story, for what reason I can't imagine."

Sometimes the truth was best. "I did wonder," I said, "and we did rummage through your house as you suspected. I found a perfectly good Santa outfit upstairs. Not destroyed. Boots shiny. Want to explain?"

"I can start there as well as any place," Bob said, "and I can show you the original Santa outfit in shreds—I've kept it in a locked shed outside. Thought it might be evidence . . . if something did happen to me."

"The one I saw was what the Menescotta community made for you?" I asked.

"Didn't have time to get to it yet, so I told them not to bother. My daughter, Anise, made that for me. She brought it yesterday. That's where I'll start the story once Maude pours me another cup of coffee."

# 10

We sat around Bob's dinette set while Maude poured us all a cup of coffee. She found a bowl of sugar and placed it on the table. Bob brought out a pitcher of cream from the refrigerator before he sat down with us.

Bob touched Maude's hand as she reached for his cup.

"Thanks, sweet Maude," he said. "Pour yourself a cup and sit with us. Try some fresh cream. There's nothing like it."

He stood and insisted Maude take his seat. Then he brought over a straight-backed chair from the corner of the kitchen and sat beside her. "It's rare I have more people visiting me than I can fit around this table. Ruth always wanted a bigger table in here, but I couldn't see the need. You think I should get one, Maude?"

"Not my house, Bob," Maude said. "You should have it the way you like it."

Bob smiled and put one arm over the back of Maude's chair. He looked completely at ease.

Did he have some kind of mother fixation? Like a puppy that wasn't weaned properly? Maude was a lovely woman, but she looked her age or close enough to it. Bob was at least twenty years younger.

"The story," I said.

"Anise came to visit me yesterday. It was a complete surprise. She brought a new Santa costume and said I mustn't give up my role as town Santa. It meant so much to the children, really to everyone in Menescotta, she told me. Anise said she'd gotten emails from friends still living in Menescotta who'd heard the rumors that I might not be Santa this year. They told her what had happened to my Santa suit."

"You hadn't told her?" I asked.

"Didn't want to bother her, and we hadn't parted on the best of terms after the wedding. That was Albert's fault, as usual. I thanked her for the suit—it's beautiful—but I also told her not everyone wanted me in that role—obviously. Anise wouldn't take no for an answer."

He took another sip of coffee. "Good!" he said to Maude. "You make it just the way Ruth always made it. Strong."

I sighed loudly, and I think Bob got the point.

"The story," he said nodding at me. "Anise said she had thoughts about what was going on. Albert had been staying with them for months, helping Anise's husband with the crop. Then he'd been gone a few weeks saying he had business to attend to. When Anise heard about the Santa suit being shredded she had it out with Albert. She thought he might be involved."

"Albert is in town?" I asked.

Bob ignored my question. "Anise said her brother denied cutting up the Santa outfit or letting the horses out of the barn. Albert apparently denied all of it. 'Course he didn't get in touch with me. He left it to Anise to tell me. Albert's always been a coward."

"So was he in town?" I asked again.

"Someone thought they'd spotted him on Main Street.

They asked if he was staying with me. I said I hadn't spoken to him since Anise's wedding."

"And that conversation hadn't gone well," I said.

"No," Bob said.

"Want to tell us about it?" I asked.

"No. Any conversation I have with Albert always ends up in a shouting match."

"Why did Anise think he could have been involved?" I asked.

"She knew he was still mad at me," Bob said, "newly mad from the wedding. Albert claimed all I cared about was myself and my land. I pretended to be this good guy when I put on my Santa suit, but I wasn't."

"Did Albert know you thought he was a coward?" Maude asked softly.

Bob shrugged. "Ruth said I was always too hard on him, that I favored Anise. Anise was easy to love, sweet, kind, a lot like her mother. Albert was stubborn from the time he was born. If I wanted him to do one thing, he'd do the opposite. Ruth managed him better than I did. Then she died, and Albert wouldn't have anything more to do with me. He took off, you know that."

"He left home right after your wife died?" I asked.

"A few months later when Beatrice came on the scene. She said I was coddling both children. I should send them away to boarding school. That would make a man out of Albert and help Anise grow up. I think Beatrice didn't like the special relationship I had with Anise. I think she was jealous. As for Albert, I did think a military school might make a man out of him. We'd had that discussion months before Ruth died. She'd put her foot down and said she wouldn't allow it, but Albert thought Beatrice and I might make him go."

"So that's why he left?" I asked.

Bob was silent. "There was more to it than that," he finally said.

I looked at Bob and waited.

"I'm not talking about it, not now. Albert didn't believe that his mother's fall was accidental. I couldn't prove it to him, and I'm not going to try to prove it to you."

"So he left," Maude said.

Bob nodded.

"I can understand why *he* left," Maude said, "but why did Anise leave?"

"I think she believed Albert needed her more than I did, and she knew how much Beatrice disliked her. Even I could see that. Whenever Anise tried to spend time with me, Beatrice would send her off to do chores, anything to get her away from me. That's what finally destroyed my relationship with Beatrice.

"The kids were gone, and I didn't know where they were. I heard they were safe, but they were only fifteen and sixteen. Beatrice seemed gleeful about it. I guess that's what put me onto her—that and what a few people said about her, like Cora for one. Cora said she couldn't be trusted, that she was after my money. I told Beatrice to go, and I made up the story that she couldn't live in a small town like Menescotta."

"It doesn't sound like a total lie," Kate said. "Perhaps it was more that a small town like Menescotta couldn't put up with her."

Bob nodded. "The men hated to see her go—like Charlie here—but the women were delighted."

Charlie colored slightly. "She could charm a man, almost any man," he said.

"Did she charm you?" I asked.

"I admit it, she did," Charlie said. "I've never been unfaithful to Cora, but that woman tempted me."

I looked at Charlie. He was still a good-looking man at fifty something. I'd bet he was real eye candy at thirty, and Cora made it sound as if Charlie had an interest in beautiful women. "Never unfaithful? So you resisted her charms?"

"Don't bring me into the middle of this," Charlie said. "I wasn't unfaithful, and I'd never hurt Bob or Cora in that way."

Kate looked at me with that look that said I'd gone too far. "Back to the story," she said. "Do you know where the kids went?"

"One of Anise's friends called me a day or two after they left to say Anise and Albert were safe. She claimed she didn't know where they were but I was not to worry. I finally heard from Ruth's sister that they were staying with her. She said they'd move on if I tried to contact them. So, I stayed away. Once I knew they were with her, I could live with that, but I was miserable. I'd lost Ruth, and now I'd lost Anise as well."

"You didn't mention Albert," Maude said. "You didn't miss your only son?"

"Sure, I missed him. But he'd made it clear he was done with me when he was a teenager. He wasn't going to be a farmer in some podunk town. He was going away to college to become a writer, maybe a teacher. Always into his books, that boy. Never into action. He said hunting was barbaric, and that I was barbaric. We had a terrible fight when he was fifteen. He was strong enough to overpower me and he did. Ruth intervened. If she hadn't I swear one of us would have killed the other."

"He doesn't sound like a coward, Bob," Maude said. "Why did you think that about him?"

"I wanted to send him to a military school, and he refused. He said he wouldn't become a brute like me. He wouldn't go off to learn to kill people. That's when I called him a coward. I'd done my time for my country. He said there were other ways to serve. Ruth sided with him, the way she always did, and then she died a week later."

“Ruth,” Maude said, “the love of your life.”

Bob was quiet. He looked at Maude. “You are so much like her. You know what I’m thinking, what I’m feeling. I went crazy after she died. Albert questioned me about what happened the morning she fell. He thought it wasn’t an accident, and he didn’t believe my version of events.”

Why?” I asked. “What was your version of events?”

# 11

Bob sat drinking his coffee as if he wasn't going to answer my question. I stared at him and waited.

"There was so much bad blood between my son and me by then," he said. "I think he needed someone to blame for Ruth's death. Ruth was careful on the paths. She never took risks, never went out if she thought the day might turn stormy."

"Was it stormy that day?" Kate asked.

"No, and there hadn't been rain in a week. In fact, it was too dry. We needed rain for the crops. It was a sunny, cloudless day, and the path she chose was one she walked frequently. No surprises. No dangers."

"Why would Albert think you were involved with his mother's death?" Maude asked.

"Albert knew about my anger—it was exactly like his. I was away that morning, and Albert thought I must have been following her."

"Why?" Maude asked.

"It wasn't that I didn't trust her," Bob said and stared into his empty cup. Maude offered him a refill but he shook his head. "She'd started to pull away from me, and I couldn't understand why. She said I wasn't the man she married and that she wanted that man back. I thought . . . I thought maybe she'd found someone else."

"So you did follow her that morning," I said.

Bob was silent. He looked around the room and stared at Charlie.

Charlie gave him a questioning look. "What?"

"I admit I followed her. I couldn't help myself. Ruth and I had always trusted one another, but in the weeks before her death, everything changed. Albert got more and more out of control, rebellious. Ruth didn't want to have much to do with me. She said I was the problem, not Albert. I wasn't letting him find his way, that all boys rebelled when they were his age. Half the time she slept downstairs, saying she couldn't sleep and wanted to watch TV. So, yes, I followed her that morning."

"All the way to where she fell?" Maude asked softly.

Bob nodded and kept his head down.

"Did you talk to her?" Maude asked.

This time Bob shook his head. "No."

He looked directly at Charlie.

"I saw she was with someone, so I stayed back. She was with you, Charlie."

"You have that wrong, Bob. I wasn't there."

"I saw your jacket. The one you used to wear when we went hunting. Bright enough to make sure no one shot you by mistake."

"It wasn't me, Bob," Charlie said again. "You kept this to yourself all these years—this misunderstanding?"

"I saw the person I thought was you walk away, and I did the same. I planned to ask Ruth about it later, but she never came home. The next thing I knew someone notified the police that they'd found her body at the foot of the cliff and that she was dead." Bob stopped talking. He picked up his coffee cup and rinsed it in the sink. He stood with his back to us. "I don't want to talk about this anymore."

Charlie hadn't said a word, but he looked pale.

"What are you thinking, Charlie?" I asked.

"Nothing," he said. It was clear he didn't mean that.

"What is it you're not saying," I asked.

"Cora loved that jacket. She wore it more than I did, and sometimes she and Ruth would walk together. I think maybe you saw her on that path, Bob, and thought it was me."

Before he could say more, a young woman burst into the kitchen.

"Guests," she said smiling. "I saw the truck, so I knew Charlie was here. And you must be from ODPA. I love the name and the idea that women detectives will be protecting my father."

"Anise," I said.

"Yes." She shook hands with each of us as we told her our names.

"Bessie is a great horse, Dad. She did well in the snow. I was very careful with her, of course."

So that was why Bob wasn't worried about Bessie—he knew Anise had taken her out for a ride.

"Where's Addy?" Anise asked, "and why do you all look so glum?"

"Sit down, Anise," Bob said. He stood and motioned toward the empty seat beside Maude.

"Coffee?" Maude asked.

"I'll get it," Anise said. "You don't have to wait on me—just keep Dad safe."

"He seems to think he is safe," I said. "Was it something you told him?"

"Maybe." Anise poured herself a cup of coffee and sat down next to Maude. "I heard about what was going on with Dad from my aunt. She heard it from someone in Menescotta.

Things don't stay quiet even from a hundred miles away. I don't know why you didn't tell me yourself, Dad."

"I didn't want to burden you," Bob said. "You'd just gotten married, and you and I weren't doing so well. Albert stirred up trouble—the way he always likes to stir up trouble."

"Oh, Daddy," Anise said. "You still put all our fights onto Albert. It was the way you treated my husband that set me off. You made him feel like a second-class citizen, as if he wasn't good enough for me." She put a hand on his arm. "It's over now. I explained to him that you wouldn't think anyone was good enough for me and that you always thought you were right about everything—even the best way to grow potatoes."

She turned to the rest of us. "Once I heard what had happened, I made the Santa outfit for Dad and came down here to convince him not to give up his role. The kids would be crushed. Besides, I thought I knew who might be causing the trouble."

"Albert?" I asked.

She looked at me and then at her dad. "You told her about your fights with Albert?"

Bob nodded. "Had to. They asked me."

"I think it might be Albert who's behind all this," Anise said. "He's always been my protector. He denied it, but he couldn't account for where he'd been in the past week. He's living with us—Caleb and me— until he gets on his feet again."

"Gets on his feet again?" I asked.

She stared at me and smiled. "You're the one who asks all the direct questions. Dad told me about you. It sounds like he didn't tell you Albert spent six months in jail for aggravated assault. He has Dad's temper—I think that's why they never got along, too much alike and too quick to jump to conclusions. Albert thought some guy was scoping out our farm, looking for trouble. He beat the—" she hesitated.

"We're grown women, here," Kate said. "You don't have to be polite. You should hear what Flo says when she speaks freely."

Anise laughed. "So I've heard." Then she grew serious. "Let's just say he beat the guy up pretty badly, sent him to the hospital. The guy was some kind of surveyor and worked for the state of Maine. Albert thought his uniform was fake, but it wasn't. I think that uniform got Albert thinking about Dad—how Dad put on a Santa costume once a year and acted like he was everyone's friend. Albert told me how angry he was about that. He said Dad couldn't love his own children—only strangers and only once a year."

Bob winced.

"Sorry, Dad. Anyway, Albert had a lot of time to think in jail and remember old wounds. I think that when he got out, he snuck into your house when you weren't there and destroyed your outfit."

"And the arrow that wounded your father's face?" Kate asked.

"Albert was great at any sport he tried, including archery. He came close to making the Olympic team," Anise said. "So yes, I think he could have grazed my father's face. But he'd never kill Dad, never."

"Would he kill one of your father's horses to get back at him?" Kate asked.

"What do you mean?"

"You wanted to know where Addy was," I said. "She's at the vet's, an arrow in her side."

"She'll be all right," Bob said. "They might keep her a few days there to make sure there's no infection, but the arrow didn't hit any vital organs. Albert would know how to do that."

Anise's rosy face turned white.

"Albert would never harm an animal. You remember how much he hated hunting, Dad. No, Albert didn't do this. Albert said he was innocent of everything, and I didn't believe him. I told him I was going to spend time with Dad and he needed to stay away. He agreed to that and said he'd be happy never to see you again."

Anise seemed to have the same brutal honesty I was accused of having. I wondered if beneath that warm farm-girl demeanor she took some pleasure in putting her father in his place.

She saw me staring at her. "You think I'm being too hard on Dad?" she asked. "I'm telling the truth, that's all. Albert has a lot to be mad about, but he'd never actually harm Dad or any of his animals."

"Will Albert talk to us?" Maude asked. "Maybe we could meet him somewhere away from the farm and the bad blood."

"He might agree to that if I ask him to. He might if he knows Dad's life is really in danger."

Anise turned to her father. "This is serious, Dad. I had no idea."

Bob yawned. He actually yawned.

"You still think this is no big deal?" I asked.

Maude put it more gently. "Someone may want to do more than destroy your plans for Christmas or harm one of your animals. They may want to hurt you."

I was more blunt. "I don't want a dead Santa on our hands. Capeesh?"

I could feel four pairs of eyes staring at me and not pleasantly I might add.

Bob drew himself up—back straight as if he were still a military man. "I've done everything you asked of me, Flo. What more do you want? I've decided I'm not giving up my Santa gig. It's the one time I feel like a human being, like I belong in this community, like I'm important to Menescotta. I won't be bullied out of doing this. I'll keep my animals safe, and I know how to protect myself as well. "

"You didn't do such a good job with that arrow that could have taken off half your face," I said. There were times when it was important to be blunt. I didn't look around to see how others were reacting.

"We aren't asking you to give up on being Santa," I said. "We're asking you to take care, to always have one of us around, to tell us if you're going anywhere, so we can go with you."

"You're putting me in jail," Bob said.

"Jail seemed to help Albert in the end," Anise said. "I admit he came out still angry at you. But he also told me he'd mixed with some folks who had really rotten lives, and he didn't want to become one of them. He wanted to turn his life around. So 'jail' as you call it, might be the best thing for you."

"And it might keep you alive," Maude said.

# 12

Bob looked at Maude. "You seem to care if I live or die, Maude."

"I do," she said. "We all do."

"I'll follow directions for you, Maude."

Oh, no, was what I thought and didn't say. In the midst of all of this, Bob was making a play for Maude. Had he been watching the old seventies movie *Harold and Maude*?

Back to business.

"Then you'll do what we say?" I asked. "One of us will need to be with you at all times."

"Agreed," Bob said. "How about Maude?'

"No," I said. "It will be someone who knows how to use a gun—that would be Kate or me."

Bob looked disappointed and then nodded. "All right."

"Where do we start?" Anise asked. "I'm not going anywhere until the Christmas festivities are over, and I know Dad is safe. I'm on the team. My husband knows I might stay awhile. He'll come down for Christmas Day, so, what's next?"

"I think we need to talk to Albert face to face," I said, "and we need to get the list of men in your hunting club."

"Men?" Bob said. "They're not all men, just so you know."

"Whatever. We need the list and we need it now."

I turned to Charlie. "I think we need to talk with Cora about the other matter."

"Other matter?" Anise asked.

"We were talking about the day your mother died before you came in," I said. "Your father said he followed your mother that day and saw her talking to someone before she fell. He thought it was Charlie. Charlie says it was probably Cora."

"You're not suggesting either of them killed my mother?" she said. She looked horrified. "Charlie and Cora were always my parents' best friends."

"I'm not suggesting anything," I said. "We need the facts, that's all. Maybe Ruth's death has nothing to do with what's going on, but we need to find out—if we can—what happened that day. It was a clear, dry, sunny morning, and your mother was an experienced hiker. Your father said she never took risks."

"That's all true," Anise said. I thought she might cry. "It's old history, painful history. Do you really need to dredge it up again? You can't honestly believe that someone killed my mother and waited twenty years to come after my father."

"It's farfetched," I said, "but I don't want to leave anything unexplored. We don't know who is threatening your father or why. Let's start with your brother and get him off our suspect list if we can. You seem certain he's not involved."

"I am now. I'll contact him."

She left the table.

Kate turned to Bob and Charlie. She pushed a blank piece of paper and a pen in their direction. "Which one of you wants to give us the list of members in your hunting club?"

Bob shoved the paper towards Charlie.

"But I haven't notified them," Charlie said.

"We'll do that for you," Kate said. "Someone wounded

Bob's horse with an arrow. Don't you want to know who did that?"

That was enough to get Charlie to start writing.

Anise returned to the table as he was finishing up.

"Albert will meet us in Portland for breakfast tomorrow at Proud Mary Cafe. Dad, you're not invited. I'm sorry."

My stomach growled, and I looked at my watch. We'd been sitting at the kitchen table for almost two hours, drinking coffee, eating nothing. It was nearing lunch time by my calculation and my stomach's.

"Is there a place we can have lunch in Menescotta?" I asked. "A place where the locals go? I'd like to see what people know about your situation, Bob. See what people are saying about it."

Bob grunted. "Everyone will know about it but no one will say anything. You'll see. People have nothing better to do in the winter than gossip among themselves. They'll talk about the weather, but they won't ask any personal questions about my situation. We Mainers know a lot, but we don't say a lot, especially to strangers. That's one reason I like living here."

"Nonetheless, I want to take a look at the town and the people in it," I said. "Whoever is doing this is someone who knows you and your habits and what will get to you."

"What Flo really means is that she's hungry," Kate said. "Best we feed her."

"I'm hungry, too," Maude said, "and I want to see the town."

"Charlie, can you come?" I asked. "And invite Cora." It wasn't so much a request as a command. Charlie seemed to get the message.

"We'll meet you there," Charlie said. "At the River Lodge. You'll see all the regulars there and get good food. One o'clock?"

"Could we make it twelve?" I asked.

"I told you Flo was starving," Kate said and smiled at me.

I didn't smile back. "It's good to have a routine and stick to it. Regular meals at regular hours."

"Right," Kate said. "Along with regular snacks."

Everyone smiled at that except me.

"I'm not coming," Bob said. "You'll hear more if I'm not around, and I've got work to do. No one's going to attack me in the middle of the day, and besides I'll take Elsie with me wherever I go."

Carrying around his rifle didn't sound reassuring to me, but Maude intervened.

"We're going to worry about you," Maude said. "Could you stay inside while we're gone?"

Bob sighed. "Okay, Maude, I'll do that for you. I got some work I can do in the house, but don't stay away too long."

Did he wink at her? I was pretty sure he winked at her. Good lord.

"Call us if you need us," Kate said.

Bob grunted something in reply.

We agreed to meet at noon at the River Lodge.

The River Lodge was clearly a local hangout. No reservations, which meant we had to wait half an hour to find seating for the six of us at the one large table in the center of the room. I always carry my own bag of trail mix, so I managed to sustain myself.

There were twenty men in the small restaurant. I wondered where the women were and asked about that.

"It's more of a guy's place," Anise explained. "Hunters love it."

I glanced around the walls made of plank wood, which were covered with animal heads and all kinds of guns.

"It has a kind of cabin-in-the-woods vibe," Kate said. "I like it."

"I thought it might be a natural place to meet some members of our hunting club," Charlie said. "Wouldn't seem so suspicious."

Kate and I walked slowly around the room as if we were actually interested in what was hanging on the walls—a moose head, a massive deer head with antlers next to what appeared to be antique rifles. She chatted about the heads and guns while I searched the faces of the men settled at the tables. A few men gave Kate the once over—she was a good-looking woman after all. She smiled back at them. Normally, she would have shot them her dead-man stare. Let me rephrase that—the stare that said if you keep looking at my body the way you are, you'll be a dead man. This time she gave them a look that said she was pleased they noticed her. We'd orchestrated all of this before we'd left for lunch.

Maude would keep herself seated next to Cora and Charlie. She wouldn't bring up anything controversial, but she'd listen. And if the opportunity arose, she'd ask a few questions —the way only Maude could. If we gave her enough time, she'd have everyone's life story including perhaps what happened the morning Ruth died.

Kate and I would get the lay of the land, see who noticed Cora and Charlie and perhaps the absence of Bob. We hadn't made it around the room when we saw a young man approach Anise. She was seated next to Charlie in a long row of chairs near the cash register.

"Hey, Anise, Charlie," the man said.

Charlie nodded at us and mouthed the words, "Hunting Club."

Kate and I moved closer, near enough to hear the conversation.

Anise held out her hand. "Hey, Hank. How are you? I haven't seen you in ages."

"Still here. Still getting over you, if you wanna know the truth. Where's Al? He with you? I saw him the other day, but he took off before I could talk to him."

"Where'd you see him?" Anise asked.

"In town. You sound surprised. He was in the seed and feed store. I assumed he was buying supplies for your dad. I thought they must have made amends. Are you both living here now?"

"Nope," Anise said. "I'm visiting for the holidays. I guess you heard about what happened to my dad."

"Naw. Bet he's happy to have you back in town."

"You haven't heard about the troubles he's had?" she asked. "The Santa costume that got destroyed? The intruder he saw near his barn? You didn't hear about his horse Addy being wounded with an arrow? Dad almost got wounded by one as well."

Hank shook his head. "No. None of that."

"That's hard to believe, Hank. You always knew about everything going on in town. What's happened to the rumor mill?"

Hank scratched his blond head, maybe fumbling for time. "I mean I heard Bob might not be Santa this year, but I thought maybe he was tired of the whole thing."

"Nope," Anise said. "He'll be at it again this year, and I'll be at his side. You hear about anyone stirring up trouble, you let me know."

"Sure. I heard you got married a month ago. That broke my heart."

Anise punched him in the shoulder. "You only cared about the one who got away. You loved the chase."

Hank grinned at her. "You could always see through me, but I'm settled now. Married, two kids."

She smiled back at him. "You still a member of Dad's hunting club?"

"Gave that up when they turned to bows and arrows, not my thing. I figured they'd get tired of it and go back to using guns. How you gonna kill a moose with a bow and arrow?"

"You know the men in the club now?" Anise asked.

"Sure." He took a step back from Anise. "Wait a sec. You think one of those guys took a shot at your dad and his horse?" He seemed to get agitated. "Those men are my friends. Bob's too. No one in Menescotta would do that! You've been away too long if you think that might happen."

Time to rescue Anise. Kate and I walked up to her.

"Looks as if the people are leaving the big table," I said.

Kate introduced herself. "I'm Kate, an old friend of Anise's, and this is my grandmother, Flo."

I hated it when she did that. She only did it to needle me.

Hank looked at both of us. "I know who you are. You're not some old friend. You're part of the old biddies detective group. It's all over town who you are. Good for a laugh."

Kate reddened and started to speak. I stood in front of her and put my face very close to Hank's. "We are from ODPA, the Old Dames Protection Agency. If you know about us then you must know why we're here. Why don't you stop lying and help us out?"

"We protect our own," Hank said. "We don't like outsiders getting in our business. If Bob needed protection, he could have gone to the police or to any one of us. We'd have helped him out. But I don't rat on my friends, and I don't like old biddies pretending to be cops. You could get hurt that way."

Now Kate intervened. "Are you threatening us?"

"You ain't no biddy. I'm not threatening you."

"I'm a member of ODPA," Kate said, "and I carry a gun. You should know I'll be with Bob throughout the holiday season. Tell that to your friends who might be wondering."

Hank turned red. "You're all crazy," he said and joined the friends he'd left—a group of thirty-somethings. They looked rough around the edges and they laughed as Hank leaned in to tell them his version of events.

"Hank won't be telling them the truth," Anise said. "He'd never admit he was cowed by a woman." She looked at Kate. "Do you really have a gun? On you?"

Kate patted her coat pocket. "Always."

"I don't know whether to be happy about that or scared," Anise said.

"I've never killed anyone if that's what you're worried about, but it does make people sit up and take notice."

"That was quite a conversation you had, Anise," I said. "A good one. Now, we know Hank—and likely everyone else in town—has heard the rumors. And we also know it's unlikely any of the men will talk to us. Will the women feel the same way?"

"Not all, I think," Anise said. "Cora has good friends here and so do I."

"Let's have lunch and then we may want to talk to some wives of the men in the bow-and- arrow club."

# 13

The River Lodge provided us with a tasty lunch, and the atmosphere was cozy if a little loud. We felt as if we were gathered in a log cabin in the woods. A wood-burning fireplace roared in one corner. It was almost too hot for a small place like this, and I noticed an open window beside the fireplace. Outside I could see more snow falling.

Men were talking and laughing all around us. A few looked furtively in our direction but we kept our focus on the food. I did anyway.

I had lobster mac and cheese. Anise, Maude and Cora had clam chowder. Kate tried the French meat pie, a cousin of Shepherd's Pie, and Charlie settled on a hamburger. We didn't speak until most of the lunch crowd had left, and even then we kept our voices down.

"How well do you know Hank?" I asked Anise.

"We went to high school together before Albert and I moved away. He was always full of himself, football star, that sort of thing. If you're asking whether or not he could be the one threatening my father, the answer is no. He's a big talker, that's all, and he doesn't have a beef with Dad."

"He wasn't a big talker this morning," I said, "and people change. Have you seen him since you left town as a teenager?"

Anise shook her head. "I heard about him through my girlfriends who stayed here. I knew when he got married and had kids, that sort of thing."

"Then he goes on our list," I said. "He didn't tell us the truth about what he knew, and he sounded angry."

"I know Hank's mom," Cora said. "She'll tell me what's going on with Hank, and she may know about the newer members of the bow-and-arrow club."

Kate got the details on Hank's mother and promised not to contact her until Cora had spoken with her.

"I'll give her a call now if you like," Cora said. She left the table and stepped outside to make her call.

The waitress stopped at the table. She looked to be in her late teens or early twenties, a cute girl with her light-brown hair pulled back in a ponytail. I wondered if this was where she'd work for the rest of her life. She smiled as if she were completely content with whatever life might have in store for her. She asked if we wanted dessert. We declined.

"You can sit here as long as you like," she said. "Lunch rush is over." She stood at our table a minute longer. "You really should try our Indian Pudding." She said that loud enough for her manager to hear. Then, she spoke softly. "I heard about what happened to Bob. Everyone in town knows about the shredded outfit, no matter what they say. He was always the best part of Christmas to me. He let me sit on his lap when I was a little kid and pull on his beard. I think I know who may be behind this."

"I would like to try one serving of the Indian Pudding," I said. I raised my voice the way some older people do who are hard of hearing. "Sounds delicious."

Our waitress scribbled on her pad, and then ripped off both copies and handed them to me.

"We'll make this on the house," she said. "My treat."

I took the sheets and folded them over. "We won't get you in trouble," I whispered.

She smiled. "No worries. My dad owns the place, and I'm only here for the holidays. Then it's back to college."

I blushed. I hated to admit it, but sometimes my assumptions about people were way off base.

She left and I unfolded the papers and read what she wrote. *"Rudolph Samson. Always had it in for Bob and knows how to use a bow and arrow."*

Cora returned to the table as I was reading the note. "No luck," she said. "Hank's mother and father have gone to Florida for the winter and won't be back until May. We may run into that problem a lot. Many of my friends have become snowbirds—they no longer like our long cold winters. What about your friends, Anise?"

"Lots have moved away, and I lost touch with many others when I left."

"Too bad," I said. "Well, here's what I've got from our very forthcoming waitress," I said. I kept my voice low and read the note.

"Didn't we hear about Rudolph Samson from Bob?' I asked. "He certainly has the right name for a holiday kill," I said.

"Except that Rudolph was a good reindeer," Maude said, "the best reindeer."

"Tell me what you know about Rudolph Samson," I said, looking at Cora and Charlie.

"Rudolph is a big name around here," Cora said. "He owns half of the land around Menescotta, and Bob owns the rest."

"He's an off-and-on member of our hunting club," Charlie said. "I'd see him at a few meetings. Can't recall that he ever actually hunted with a bow and arrow. He's the type that would use an AK-15 to kill a deer."

"AK-15?" Kate asked. "That's the latest assault rifle, isn't it?"

"Top of the line. Rudolph always has to have the top of the line." Charlie said.

"So what's he doing in the hunting club?" I asked.

Charlie shrugged. "He always pays his dues, and I imagine he belongs for business reasons. Maybe he hopes some of the older folks in the group will retire some place warm and sell their farms to him. I think he has in mind some kind of farming conglomerate. Once his plans for Walmart fell through he's been looking for other ways to get more land and make more money. He's our local banker. You want a loan, you have to go through him. Nobody likes him, but he's too powerful to have as an enemy."

"He sounds more like the one who should be stalked and threatened," I said, "than the other way around."

"He does," Cora said, "but people are afraid of Rudolph Samson. They steer clear of him. Everybody but Bob, that is. Bob confronts him every chance he gets. You heard how Bob scuttled his plans to bring a Walmart to town and then he helped defeat Samson in his run for Selectman."

"That must have infuriated him," Kate said, "and Bob's troubles started not long afterwards."

"Yes," Cora said, "but to kill a man over an election that didn't go his way, that seems extreme."

"Hmmm," I said.

I looked over at Kate.

"He's already on the list," she said, "but I think we need to bump him up a little higher."

Our cute waitress brought our Indian Pudding along with several small bowls and spoons. I mouthed a thank you to her. Then we took our time. I spooned out the Indian Pudding in slow motion hoping the last of the lunch crowd would leave. We each ate one or two bites.

It was a remarkably delicious custard with cornmeal, raisins and holiday spices, and I would have been content to finish the whole bowl. However, Kate put a hand on my arm and nodded in the direction of the now empty restaurant. I put down my spoon.

"I want to come back to something," I said, "something better discussed away from Bob. It's about the day Ruth died and the person Bob saw."

"You want to know who was wearing Charlie's jacket, talking to Ruth before she fell off that cliff," Cora said. "I was. It's ancient history. I can't see it having anything to do with what's happening now, but we can talk about it."

She sounded a little defensive to my ear. "Do you mind, Anise if we talk about it?" I asked.

"I don't mind. I want to hear."

"I often walked with Ruth," Cora said. "We were very close. That day, I said I'd catch up with her after I did a few chores. That's what happened. We talked a little and then I said I had to go back home. We had a cow ready to give birth, and Charlie and I both needed to be there. I wish I'd stayed a little longer. Maybe I could have prevented a tragedy. I never saw Bob."

"That's it?" I asked.

"That's it," Cora said. "I didn't push her off a cliff if that's what you're imagining. She was my best friend."

Anise had been very quiet. Now, she leaned forward. "She was your best friend until your falling out a few days before Mom died. Mom didn't tell me much about it, only how sad she was to lose her best friend. I was fifteen at the time, and I think she told me because I'd just had a big fight with my best friend."

"What was the fight all about between you and Ruth?" Maude asked Cora.

I was glad she stepped in. I would have confronted Cora with the fact she'd been lying to us. I knew Maude's way was the better one. More flies with honey, that sort of thing. I sat back and let Maude nurse along this conversation.

# 14

Cora looked at Maude. "It was horrible. I never wanted to distrust her, but I think I got caught up in Bob's worries. He was afraid Ruth was going to leave him and that maybe she'd already found someone else. I worried it might be Charlie."

Charlie started to say something and then shook his head.

Cora sighed.

"I know what you've always said, Charlie, that you like to look, that all men like to look. But I also knew we'd married in our prime. You were twenty-five and I was thirty-five. The age difference didn't matter much then to either one of us, but ten years later I thought it might. The four of us used to take long rides together. Then it seemed to become you and Ruth who spent time together, riding and hiking. I guess I let my imagination run away with me. I tried to talk to Ruth about it, but she got so insulted. She said best friends should trust one another."

Charlie put a hand out as if to stop Cora from saying more.

"I believe you, Charlie, but I didn't at the time. There were too many circumstances where you weren't home, and I didn't know where you were. Menescotta gossips filled in the gaps—that you and Ruth went hiking and stayed in the woods for hours when you were together. That's why I really followed Ruth. I wanted to see for myself. The only person I found was Ruth. I decided that was as good a time as any to have it out with her. We'd be alone where no one could hear what we had to say."

"You thought my mother was having an affair," Anise asked, clearly shocked, "with Charlie?"

"It happens. Your mother was younger than I was and beautiful. Ruth denied it, of course. She got angry and upset and told me to go away. An hour later I found out she'd fallen to her death. I've felt guilty ever since. Maybe she wasn't paying attention to the path because of me."

"I'm sorry you had so many doubts about us," Charlie said. "You want to know what Ruth and I did while we hiked?"

Cora kept her head down but nodded.

"We talked about our jealous spouses, that's what we talked about. We couldn't find a way to convince either one of you how little you had to worry about. Ruth was like a sister to me—nothing more than that and nothing less. You were so consumed with the children. Sometimes, I needed to get away—never from you, but from all the responsibilities. Maybe in that way it mattered that I was younger than you. I wasn't very mature back then."

No one had anything to say after that. We couldn't eat any more of our Indian Pudding.

Our waitress came over to see if we were all right. I told her we were too full of lunch to eat dessert, and she said she'd box it up for us. She winked at me but didn't say another word. It wasn't until we got home that I found the note in the box, addressed to me. I took it up to my room and told Maude and Kate to join me.

*"I couldn't say more at the table,"* she wrote. *"Not with Anise there.*

*But I thought you should know. I saw Rudolph Samson outside the restaurant as I was closing up a few days ago. He was talking to someone who stood in the shadows. I couldn't see him clearly but he had the same round face Anise has and the same blond hair. Neither one of them saw me, but I heard part of their conversation. 'That old man needs to be taught a lesson,' Rudolph Samson said. 'A permanent one,' the younger man replied."*

"Oh, no," Maude said. "Albert!"

"You think Albert will show tomorrow morning?" Kate asked.

"That's anyone's guess," I said, "but regardless, we need to find out from Anise what the real story is between Albert and Bob."

We took the note downstairs and found Cora who was busy cleaning up the kitchen.

"Can we help?" Kate asked.

Naturally, I was relieved when Cora said no. While I didn't mind causing trouble, I hated to be the one who had to clean it up.

"Our waitress left this for us," I said.

Cora read the note. "Anise will be very upset if she reads this. She thinks her brother walks on water. She knows he has a temper like his dad, but she continues to claim he's turning over a new leaf. She has an affliction of only seeing the good in Albert."

"So this note doesn't surprise you?" Maude asked.

"It disappoints me. Sometimes the men in this town act like they're still in grade school."

"It doesn't worry you?" I asked. "You don't take it seriously?"

"I didn't take it seriously until Bob's horse Addy got hurt. Is she doing okay?"

"Yes," Kate said. "Last I heard she was doing fine."

"We don't hurt our animals in Menescotta to make a

point," Cora said. "To answer your question, Flo, I am getting more and more worried. Things seem to be getting worse for Bob. The Santa suit was cut and shredded in such a violent way, it scared me. That's why I agreed to let my mom contact you. And now with this attack on Bob and his horses—I'm glad you're here."

"You think Rudolph and Albert could be responsible for all this?" I asked. "You think Albert could kill his own father?"

Cora was quiet. "Albert is easily led, easily led astray I should say. As a boy he always wanted to be liked. Bob could never give him that affirmation. I don't know why. If anyone claimed to be his friend, Albert went along with them. I don't think he could actually kill his own father, but maybe if someone convinced him that some mischief would teach Bob a lesson—maybe he'd go along with that."

She dried her hands on a hand towel. "Albert never believed his mother's death was an accident."

"Did you?"

"As I said, I left Ruth so upset, I imagined she might not have been looking where she was going. It could have been my fault."

"Did you explain that to Albert?"

"I tried to, but he wouldn't listen. He kept claiming it was his father's fault, not mine. He said his father had followed his mother and then made up some cock-and-bull story to explain what happened. I asked what it was and he wouldn't tell me. All he said was that it was a flat-out lie."

Charlie walked in as we were talking, and he found us silent, standing like statues by the sink.

"Please tell me you're not rehashing old history—or if you are, perhaps I should hear about it."

"Bob thought he saw you with Ruth," I said, "the morning she died. And then he discovered it was Cora. He saw her walk away. Do you know what he did after that?"

"He told me he walked away as well, the same story he told you." Charlie shook his head. "Ruth was the love of his life. You can't possibly think he killed her."

"He was apparently worried she was going to leave him," I said.

"So he kills her? Leaves his kids motherless? Never confesses to the crime? Come on, Cora. Flo doesn't know Bob but you do. You can't believe that."

Cora was quiet. "He would never harm her intentionally," she said at last. "But perhaps in a fit of jealous rage? It's a narrow path where she fell. How do we know he didn't shake her, make her lose her balance? And you know how Bob is if he feels guilty about something. He clams up and never admits it."

Now, Charlie was silent. "Bob never told me the rest of the story. He said he walked away, but I didn't believe that. He shut down any conversation that had to do with her death. As you say, Cora, maybe that was because he felt guilty about it.

"I assumed it was because they'd argued before she died, but you make me wonder if it was more than that. To be honest, I guess I've always wondered. Ruth never said she was afraid of Bob, but she did say she worried about his anger. She was especially concerned for Albert—that one of them might kill the other in a fight. That almost happened right before she died. She'd stopped it then, but she worried that next time she might not be around to stop it."

Charlie was pacing the kitchen. He seemed to be getting more and more worked up. "If I thought Bob had killed Ruth, I don't know what I'd do."

"You told me you couldn't imagine it," Cora said. "If it was something Bob did, I don't think he could have lived with himself."

"Maybe," I said, "or maybe it's the kind of thing you

convince yourself never happened, and over time you start to believe your own lies."

"Albert never believed Bob was innocent," Charlie said. "He told me his father had come up with some crazy story to explain what happened to Ruth and that he knew Bob was lying to him. So, I got worried about what Albert might be up to when people spotted him back in town and everything started to go wrong for Bob."

Did Charlie just throw Albert under the bus? Charlie, who loved Ruth like a sister—or maybe in a different way even though he denied it. What would he do if he found out—or thought he found out—that Bob had killed her?

I began to wonder about Charlie. Cora complained he'd been gone a lot lately and hadn't kept up with chores around the house. Was that because he was busy elsewhere? Could he be involved with what was happening to Bob? Could he be trying to pin the blame on someone else, like Albert?

# 15

"We should make sure Bob's okay," I said. "We promised we'd stick close by his side, and here we are half a mile away."

"Anise has gone to check on him," Kate said. "She told me Bob always took a nap in the afternoon, and she promised to call me when he woke up. I'll head over there now. One of us should be living in the house if he can tolerate it."

"Agreed," I said. "It should probably be you."

Kate reported back that Anise agreed Kate could stay in the house. We went with her to check on Bob and help her get settled into Anise's old bedroom.

Charlie dropped us at the front door. "Call when you want to come back or if you need help," he said. "We're five minutes away."

Five minutes away could be a lifetime I thought, but Kate had her gun and we had our wits about us.

Anise met us at the door. She showed us to her room. It looked like a teenager's room with posters on the walls from singers and artists Anise undoubtedly loved years ago. "Dad never touched it after I left," she said. "He was as sentimental as Mom even though he'd never admit it."

Maude and I went back downstairs while Kate got settled. Anise returned to build a fire in the large front room. She fidgeted with the logs, rearranging them, adding more. She couldn't seem to sit still.

"This old house gets so drafty, and it's supposed to be a record low tonight."

Kate entered the room in time to hear the end of the conversation. "You show me where the wood pile is, and I can bring in plenty of wood."

"No, we can handle that," she said.

"Your dad still brings in the wood?"

She hesitated a beat too long. "His arthritis acts up, so he doesn't usually try to help."

"So who's the 'we' you were talking about?" I asked.

Anise said nothing.

"You knew Albert was in town, didn't you? Where's he staying?"

"Albert's down the road with a friend."

"Anise, what really happened that made Albert take off when he did twenty years ago?" Maude asked. "And why did you follow? It must have been about more than the Beatrice woman trying to take over the place."

Anise stopped fidgeting with the fire and sat down across from Maude. "It *was* about more than that," she said. "After Mom died, we all went to pieces in our own ways. A lot of women in town tried to mother me, and I stayed away from home a lot. I couldn't bear to see how sad Dad was. Then Beatrice arrived on the scene, and that was another reason to stay away.

"Albert remained glued to the house, as if he wanted to make sure Beatrice didn't run off with all our valuables. And then something happened. I wasn't there. I didn't see it, but

Albert and Dad had a fight that ended their relationship. Albert wouldn't tell me what happened, and he still hasn't told me much about the argument. At the time he said Dad was a liar, and he had to leave."

Anise stood and lit the fire she'd so carefully laid. It burst into flame. She remained standing with her back to it.

"I could see Albert needed me more than Dad did, so I went with him. Mom's sister took us in. I knew Dad would be worried sick about us, so I called a friend and told her to let Dad know we were safe. For weeks, Albert wouldn't let our aunt contact my father. Then, I finally convinced Albert to let her call him. Dad agreed to let us stay with our aunt."

"You really have no idea what the fight was about?" Maude asked.

Anise looked at her. "There were rumors that my mom's death wasn't an accident. They were horrible to hear and they even included the idea that Dad had taken up with Beatrice before my mom died."

"Was Beatrice in town before your mother died?" I asked.

"She worked in the bank—Rudolph Samson's bank," Anise said. "She probably came a few months before my mother died. Dad had business with the bank, and I remember he talked about this very helpful woman who worked there."

"Did you believe the rumors?" Maude asked.

"No. Dad loved my mother, sometimes too much. Sometimes, he didn't want to let her out of his sight."

"Did Albert believe the rumors?" I asked.

"I don't know. He never told me details about the argument he had with Dad except to say Dad wasn't being honest with us. I pressed him on that, and all he would say was that Dad invented a story about what happened to our mother that couldn't possibly be true."

"Do you know what the story was?" Maude asked.

"No, but Albert said he couldn't stay in the house any

longer with Dad. I told him to go and I followed. He was so upset and so angry—I couldn't let him be by himself. Albert and I are like two pieces of a whole. Like yin and yang. I needed to be by his side to calm him down and keep him from doing something he'd regret for the rest of his life."

"Anise," Maude said slowly, "what do you think happened the day your mother died, and who do you think wants to harm your father now?"

"I don't like to think about the past, and I'm not sure my mother's death has anything to do with what's happening now to my dad."

"We aren't either," I said, "but we need to sift through whatever information we can get about why someone might want to harm Bob."

I could feel a chill in the air, and I edged closer to the fire. Anise stoked it and offered me a throw. "Mom made this, and Dad could never part with it. It's almost good as new."

I took the knitted throw and wrapped it around me. "Snug and warm," I said.

Anise smiled, and when she smiled she looked the way her mother had in the picture tucked in a drawer upstairs. I was pretty sure she'd give me the shirt off her back if I asked for it.

"I understand that you have to look at everything, past and present," she said. "My mom was a good hiker. I don't see how she could have slipped. It was a clear day and the hike was one she took often. It's a narrow path, so I suppose if something startled her, she could have fallen. But I can't believe that anyone would have pushed her. Everyone loved her."

"And yet Albert thinks someone did kill your mother," I said, "and he seems to think it could have been your father."

Maude shook her head at me as if I was once again pushing too hard.

Anise sat down and stared at us with those round trusting eyes. "I don't think he believes that anymore."

"Why do you say that?" Maude asked.

"The wedding. Albert came to my wedding partly to make amends with Dad. He told me he was ready to leave the past behind. Albert couldn't know what really happened. We were in school when Mom fell, but both of us knew our parents were unhappy with each other for days before she died. They weren't speaking to one another—not any time I was around at least.

"Dad has a terrible temper and he can be a very jealous man. Somehow I think he got it in his head that Mom might leave him, but that was a ridiculous thought."

Anise stood and walked to the window. She seemed reluctant to go on with the story.

"What is it, Anise?" Maude asked.

"I think that Albert believed, maybe still believes, that Dad confronted Mom on the path. Maybe they argued. Maybe he pushed her and didn't mean to." Anise wiped a single tear from her cheek. "If Dad had done that, his guilt might have kept him from admitting it. He always had a hard time admitting he did something wrong, but he never would have harmed my mother on purpose."

"You never asked him?" I said.

"I couldn't. He was suffering more than any of us. I couldn't add to his suffering by making him think I didn't believe him—didn't believe he was completely innocent."

Anise moved toward the door. "Dad's been asleep a long time. I think I should check on him."

We heard her walk slowly up the stairs as if she had the weight of the world on her shoulders. A minute later, she came running back down.

"Dad's gone," she said. "He knew he wasn't supposed to go anywhere alone, and he ignored all of us."

Anise grabbed a coat and ran out the door. We watched her head for the barn. We grabbed our coats from the coat rack and pulled on our boots. The barn doors stood open.

Anise ran back to us, breathless. "He's taken Bessie and the sleigh. I'll bet he wanted to check things out before next week's parade. He wanted to make sure Bessie could carry him on her own with no problems."

We could see tracks from the sleigh heading away from the house.

"There's a broad field near a creek behind our house. That's probably where he went," Anise said. "I'll track him on foot. Kate, will you come with me? You two stay here."

"No, dear," Maude said. "We're going with you. Don't wait on us. We'll follow as quickly as we can."

## 16

Kate and Anise ran ahead. Maude and I moved more slowly behind. We'd be no use to anyone if either of us tripped and broke a leg. I pretended I was looking out for Maude, and I'm sure she did the same for me. We followed the path that led from the barn, and we could still see Anise and Kate marching ahead of us. Then the path turned and they disappeared behind a cluster of birch trees.

We followed the tracks of the sleigh and Bessie's hoof prints. At first, the tracks looked smooth and easy. The snow was packed down. It was nothing that should have caused any trouble, except that somehow it had.

"Look, Maude," I said, pointing to the two tracks of the sleigh. See how smooth that right track is and how bumpy the line is for the second one?"

"I do." Maude bent down to take a better look. "This runner is worn differently. It's thinner."

"And it seems to be wobbling—not the straight, smooth path like the one on the right."

We caught a glimpse of Anise and Kate again—this time they were running off the path to the left. Kate looked back and motioned us to catch up. Then we heard a scream, Anise's, I suspected. That was partly because I rarely heard Kate scream. If there was a problem she took care of it.

We followed as quickly as we could. While the snow seemed tamped down, I'd had enough experience with a sudden snow drift to recognize the potential for a broken ankle. We moved as fast as we could safely, but we'd lost the women again beyond a towering forest of white pine trees.

"Over here," Kate yelled.

We entered the wide field Anise had mentioned and saw the reason for her scream. In the center of the field, the sleigh lay on its side. Bessie stood calmly beside it. We saw no signs of Bob, but we did see Anise and Kate hovering over what looked like a round mound in the snow.

By the time we caught up with them, Anise and Kate were helping Bob stand.

"I'm all right," he said. "It's my arm, that's all. And Bessie's okay. Could have been a lot worse."

I called Charlie, who said he'd come right over. He said he knew exactly where we were.

"Should we call 911?" Maude asked. "Is it broken?" She pointed to Bob's arm which he held with his other hand.

"Charlie will be faster," Anise said, "and I think it is broken."

"What happened?" I asked.

"I could feel the sleigh pulling to the left," Bob said. "I thought Bessie wasn't used to pulling alone, so I kept nudging her back to the path. Then once we got to the open field, and I tried to maneuver the sleigh, it lurched to the left. That's when I knew I was in trouble. I loosened the harness and dropped the reins before the whole thing fell sideways. Bessie had the good sense to run off, but she came back to check on me."

"You could have been killed, Dad." Anise sounded shaken. "If the sleigh had fallen differently, it could have crushed you."

"Not likely," Bob said, "but can you imagine what it would have done to the children if they'd been watching?"

Maude shook her head. "That would have been terrible. Is there anyone around here who hates children or Christmas?"

"Or Santas?" I asked. "We've been assuming this was an attack on you personally," I said. "I still think that's the most likely explanation, but what if it was an attack on Christmas? First, the Santa suit, then the sleigh. I know you thought about that as well, Bob—that if someone wanted to kill you, they could easily have done so. Maybe this really is an effort to keep you from being in the parade as Menescotta's Santa."

"That doesn't explain the arrow that whizzed past Dad's face or the wound to Addy," Anise said.

"Maybe not," I said, "but what if the person simply wanted to put Bob out of action for a few weeks until the holiday season was over, kind of a real-life Grinch?"

"They won't get away with it," Bob said, shaking his good arm in the air. "You won't make me stop unless you kill me!" Then he moaned and grabbed his broken arm.

Charlie showed up with Cora beside him.

"What's the shouting all about?" he asked. "They probably heard you in Menescotta."

Cora saw Bob holding his arm. "Did you hurt anything else besides your arm?" she asked.

"My sleigh," Bob said, "same one I've used for fifteen years."

Charlie examined the wreckage. "Someone's tampered with this runner. See? This left one's been shaved down, notched. I'm surprised you made it this far."

Bob started to bend over to look at the runner sitting wedged in the snow.

Kate stopped him. "We need to get you to a hospital," she said. "Charlie, can you and Anise take him? We'll examine the sleigh."

"I'll call the police," Cora said.

Bob muttered something about giving publicity to the bad guy or guys who did this, but Cora shushed him. "The police have to get involved and stay involved," she said.

"Amen to that," Kate added.

"We'll stay here," I said, "until the police arrive. Maybe they can get fingerprints."

Bob scoffed at that. "They'll be lucky to find their way here, and they won't know any more than we do. They'll get no fingerprints. No nothing."

"Do you have someone in town who's a woodworker," I asked, "and might know what was done to the sleigh?"

This was said to everyone standing there.

"Yeah, plenty of them," Charlie said."I have some friends in town who could help us out."

Bob moaned and then tried to disguise it with a cough.

"We have to get my dad to a hospital," Anise said.

"You're right," I said. "Everyone in Menescotta will know what happened in an hour. Any woodworker you trust that we can get here before then?"

"There's Wyatt Miller," Cora said. "I'm surprised you didn't think of him first, Charlie. He and Bob are old friends. He might even have been the man who made this sleigh fifteen years ago."

"He did make the sleigh," Bob said.

"Then he'll know what's wrong with it."

"We'll call him from the car," Anise said. She helped her dad back to the path, and I watched as Anise and Charlie walked slowly to where their truck was parked. Cora led Bessie back to the barn.

Then we waited.

# 17

We shivered, stomped our feet and walked around the sleigh. We could feel the temperature dropping even though the sun was out.

"I can stay here," Kate said. "I don't want either of you catching pneumonia."

"I'm not going anywhere," I said.

Maude was the one who was in danger of pneumonia. She'd had a bout of it last winter.

"Why don't you go back to the house, Maude? You could look around a bit more since everyone's gone for a while."

Maude started to protest and then seemed to think better of it. "I'd have the whole house to myself," she said. "I could start in the kitchen where Bob kept the quitclaim deed. I wonder what else he might have hidden there."

"Yes! It's actually a perfect opportunity," I said. "No one will bother you for at least an hour. Do you need help getting back to the house?"

Maude gave me a look. "You don't like it when people treat you like a doddering old fool. I don't either. I'm exactly one year older than you. I've never broken a bone in my life, and I used to be a gymnast in my youth."

"A gymnast? You're making that up," I said.

"Yes, I am," she said, "but I love gymnastics in the Olympics. If I were a young girl today, that's what I'd do." She put her hands over her head as if she'd nailed a perfect landing. I was afraid she might show me a forward roll, but she didn't, thank goodness.

We watched as she walked confidently back to the path and toward the house, which was now out of view.

Then we waited. Cora joined us.

"Bessie's back in the barn," she said. "Not a thing wrong with her, fortunately."

Twenty minutes later, Anise called us. Bob had a clean break. He'd get a cast and be out of there in an hour or two. She told us Wyatt was on his way.

After another twenty minutes, an older man arrived in a truck with a snowplow on the front. His hair was long, gray and tied in the back in a low ponytail. He had a full beard and a patch over one eye. With his paunch he looked like a Santa who'd had a rough life.To be honest he was more my generation than Bob's, but while I'd taken care of myself, Wyatt looked like he'd gone out of his way not to.

"You Flo Wellington?" he asked. "Why are you staring at me? Who'd you expect? Someone fifty years younger? You're not such a spring chicken yourself. Didn't they tell you I was coming?"

He didn't seem to care I hadn't responded. I suspected he spent a lot of his time talking to himself. He kept it up as he walked slowly around the sleigh.

"Wow! I made this sleigh, you know. Made it for Robert when he was so down in the dumps after his wife died and that Beatrice woman up and took off. Did a damn good job of it, too. Look at that handlebar, that top rail—best carving I ever did."

He kept up the monologue. Kate and I followed along, looking carefully at everything he pointed to. It was beautiful carving as he said.

"Robert took care of it—kept it oiled, painted. But what's this?" He knelt to examine the runners. "Someone wanted to destroy my work or destroy Robert or both."

He stood and for the first time he stopped talking. "Where's Robert? Is he okay?"

"He's all right," Kate said. "The fall broke his arm. It looks like a clean break and they're putting a cast on."

"And Addy?" he asked.

"He was being pulled by Bessie, and she's all right. Why did you ask about Addy?"

"Robert said Addy would pull the sleigh this year like the last two years. Bessie's getting too old for that sort of thing."

"So you've been in touch with Bob recently?" I asked.

"Sure. Why?"

"You know about his troubles?" I asked.

"What troubles? We quit talking a few weeks ago when he left the hunt club. Said he'd had enough of the bow-and-arrow fiasco. I had too, frankly." He pointed to the patch on his eye. "Some damn fool tried to put my eye out. Doc says I'll be okay in a few weeks. But there's a lot I can't do with one eye—no depth perception. You can't use a bow and arrow for one thing."

"Some damn fool?" I asked.

"That's what I said. Some damn fool. Probably one of the new members. So cock sure they know everything when they know nothing at all. 'Course Bob was the one hunting with me when it happened. Denied he knew anything about what happened."

"When did it happen, Mr. Miller?" Kate asked.

"Wyatt, that's my name. We don't put on airs around here."

"Wyatt, when did that happen?" Kate asked again.

"Six weeks ago. Never did find out who was responsible. Came out of nowhere. Could have killed me. And I made the damn arrow that nearly put out my lights. Won't be doing that again."

"You really have no idea who did it?" I asked.

"Not for sure."

"And you stayed in the club after it happened?" Cora asked.

"Yeah. I like most of the guys. Gets me out of the house. Whoever did it was sorry even if they couldn't fess up to it."

He ran his hand over the bottom rail. "Someone wanted to put out Robert's lights as well. Look at this rail. It looks fine on the surface, but rub your hand on the underside."

Kate obliged. "It's rough," she said, "and gouged in places. I can feel how it narrows."

"You got that right. Someone tampered with it, so it would either break or pitch the whole sleigh onto its side first time out. Could have happened with the kids watching although not with Bob driving it. Bob always took the sleigh out for a practice run before the big day—he'd do that for sure this year if he was going to use Bessie again. She hasn't pulled that weight, any weight in the last two years. Where is Addy?"

"At the vet's," I said. "Someone shot her in her side. She'll be okay but not in time to pull the sleigh this year."

"Wow, that's bad. First Addy and now the sleigh. I can fix the sleigh—make a new runner in time for the parade next week, but if Robert has a broken arm, he can't drive this thing. That'll take two good arms even with a well-mannered horse like Bessie."

He paused and scratched his beard. "I could do it, I suppose. I don't want to see the kids disappointed."

I tried to imagine Wyatt pretending to be a jolly old Santa, and I couldn't make it work.

"What? You're doing that staring thing again. You don't think I'm fit to be Santa? Any port in a storm you know. I could do it if I had to."

"No depth perception," Kate said.

"You got a point," Wyatt admitted.

"You've given me an idea," Kate said. "Maybe I could be the elf who drives the sleigh, and Santa, Bob, could throw out candy canes or whatever. You think you can mend the runner in a week?"

"I can mend that runner in two days."

"Can you keep the whole thing quiet?" I asked. "Whoever did this will want to know what happened. I think a news blackout might bring him out into the open."

"I can do that. My house and workshop are ten miles from here, outside Menescotta. No one arrives unannounced. Got my hunting dogs, and they pick up any scent."

"And the sleigh?" I asked.

"All I need is the runner. I can detach it and carry it off with me now. Got someone to put the sleigh back in the barn? That's where Robert kept it."

"Charlie," I said, "he could do it."

Wyatt nodded. "You sure he can keep his mouth shut? He's a good guy, far as I know, but he likes to spread the news. Especially if he's been drinking."

"He told me privately he'd sworn off drinking," Kate said. "At least for the holiday season to see how it goes."

Cora gave Kate a look. "When did he tell you that?"

"When he invited me out for a drink," Kate said. "He said he'd buy me one but he'd refrain."

"And why did he invite you out for a drink?" I asked. "Did you go, Cora?"

"I wasn't invited."

"He said you were busy," Kate said, "but he had some free time and would love to show me around."

Wyatt listened to our conversation and then chuckled. "Hard to keep that horse in the paddock, isn't it, Cora? He's a boy who likes a pretty face." He looked over at Cora and saw her crestfallen expression. We all did. "You're a looker, Cora, I didn't mean to suggest your weren't. If I were a few years younger, I'd give Charlie a run for his money. I'm just saying he enjoys a *new* pretty face."

Cora nodded and looked miserable.

"He looks but doesn't touch," I said. "Isn't that the way you put it, Cora?"

"Maybe," Wyatt said. "You keep him on a pretty short leash—I'll bet that's how you keep him in line."

"I'm going home, Wyatt," Cora said. "You always like to stir up mischief. If you girls need me, call. I can walk home this way—it isn't far."

We watched her tromp off doggedly through the snow.

"You really hurt her feelings," Kate said.

"Forewarned is forearmed," Wyatt said.

"You don't like Charlie?" Kate asked.

"I like him fine. I'm just not sure what he's up to all the time. Bob thought he might have been up to something with Ruth before she died. I think maybe Cora thought that as well. Don't know if he was or if he wasn't."

Wyatt accused Charlie of spreading rumors, but he was doing a pretty good job of it on his own.

"You're making it sound like Charlie isn't trustworthy" I said.

"Not saying that exactly."

"I'm not sure what you're saying, Wyatt." This was from Kate. "If you don't think Charlie can keep quiet about what happened out here, maybe we should load the whole sleigh onto your flat bed and let you take it to your workplace. We can tell Charlie you don't know if you can get it fixed in time for the parade. Then we can spread whatever rumors we want spread."

"The sleigh's heavy. But I'm the one who built it, so I know how to dismantle it. You two run along. I'll take it from here."

"I'll stay and help," Kate said. "Flo, why don't you go back and check on Maude? The others may be getting back home soon."

Kate knew how much I hated to be told what to do, but in this case she had a point. Maude had had almost an hour to search the house, and she might have found something.

I nodded and headed out. I walked a little more carefully than Maude had. I was a lot taller than she was, farther from the ground. I was also clumsier if I was going to be honest about it. Maude might have been a great gymnast if she'd been born fifty years later.

# 18

I kept an eye on my feet and walked slowly. One broken bone in this adventure was enough. I stomped the snow off my boots at the back door of Bob's house and called to Maude as I entered.

"You look frozen," she said to me. "Here. Get out of that coat and those boots. The kitchen's warm and I'll make you a cup of tea."

"Find anything?'

Maude's eyes twinkled. "Plenty."

Before she could say more, we heard a truck in the driveway. I looked out the kitchen window. It was Charlie's truck, and three people climbed out—Charlie, Anise and Bob with his arm in a cast resting in a sling. I opened the back door for them.

Bob looked forlorn.

"Does it hurt?" I asked.

"Not much. But it means I can't drive the sleigh for the parade. Probably doesn't matter since the sleigh's been destroyed."

"I'm sorry, Bob." I said. "You'll feel better once you've gotten some rest."

"The sleigh is destroyed?" Charlie asked.

"Might be," I said. "Wyatt's going to take a look at it and let us know. We'll keep you posted."

I ushered Charlie out the door.

"You seemed in a hurry to get rid of him." Maude said.

"Bob needs to get to bed," I said. "Can I help you upstairs?"

"I got it," Bob said. "All I need is a nap, and I'll be right."

Anise took his good arm and helped him up the stairs.

"I'll check on you later," Maude said. "If you need anything, call out."

"Will do. Thanks, Maude. Ruth could hear me from anywhere in the house. I expect you're just like that."

We watched them until they were safely on the second-floor landing.

"Someone has a crush on you," I said.

"He's lonely, that's all," Maude said.

I wondered about that, but it was a problem for another day. "What have you found?"

"When I entered the house I thought I heard someone," Maude said. "I asked if anyone was here, but no one answered. I stayed in the kitchen and started looking for other tins with information in them. Twenty minutes later I heard someone on the stairs. He must have thought I'd left. Anyway, I pushed the kitchen door open slightly and saw him disappear out the front door."

"Did you get a good look at him?"

"Good enough. He was young, same hair color as Anise."

"You think it was Albert?"

"I do."

"So has he been staying in the house?" I asked. "Anise told me he was staying with a friend somewhere nearby. I wonder if she knows he's prowling around the house, and I wonder what he's been doing here. Do you think he'll actually show tomorrow and talk to us?"

Maude shook her head. "No idea, but I also found more tins of interest. I found some other documents, including a will. I don't think Bob trusts banks or lawyers."

"Was there any surprise in the will?" I asked. "I assume he left everything to Anise."

Maude pulled out the short document and pushed it in my direction. "He left most of what he had to Anise, but there was a caveat. Read it—the wording is interesting."

She pointed to the part she wanted me to read.

I pulled my reading glasses out of my pocket. I pretended to wear them because I liked how they looked on my face—like I was young and hip. I read the sentence aloud.

"*To Albert I leave one hundred thousand dollars for the love of Ruth, despite the fact he never believed me when I told him the truth about what happened.*"

I handed the paper back to Maude.

"When is the will dated?" I asked.

She looked it over. "Maybe a year after Ruth died," Maude said. "We need to get more information from Anise."

"Information about what?" Anise asked, entering the kitchen. "I see you've discovered Dad's filing system. What is it you want to know?"

"Have a seat," I said. "I think it's time you told us what happened when Albert left and you followed. The whole story this time."

Anise sank into the nearest chair. "All right," she said.

She shook off her coat and placed it on the chair behind her.

"The situation at home was horrible after Mom died," Anise said. "Beatrice came on the scene. Albert threatened to leave many times, and I said I was going with him. Then

Dad got desperate I guess. He told us he was dying, and that was a flat-out lie. We spoke to his doc who said his physical health was fine. That's when Albert had had enough. Me too. If he lied about a fake illness, maybe he'd lied about the whole encounter on the mountain. Mom was as sure-footed as a mountain goat. She didn't simply tumble off that mountain."

"So Albert left," Maude said.

"And I left with him. From a distance, we kept an eye on how Dad was doing. When Beatrice left, Dad was all gloom and doom. I thought about coming back, but I wasn't sure I could trust him. And I was afraid he'd become as possessive of me as he had been of Mom."

"You really didn't speak to him for years?" Maude asked.

"I would come for short visits at Christmas, but I kept those visits to a couple of days. I could never understand his obsession with my mother, his jealousy of anyone else she seemed to care about. Not until I met Caleb, my husband.

"Then I began to understand. When you love someone totally, you can't bear the thought of losing them. I think that's what happened to my dad. That's why I invited him to the wedding.

"I knew he couldn't kill the one person he loved above all others—my mother—no matter how angry he got at her or how afraid he was she might leave him. It was all in his head anyway. Mom loved Dad and would never have left him.

"Albert wasn't ready to reconcile. He came to believe Mom's death was an accident—I don't know why—but he still felt Dad had made her life miserable with his demands and his jealousy." Anise sighed. "I think Dad was always jealous of the special way Mom treated Albert and of the time she spent hiking with Charlie. She and Charlie loved the woods and spent hours there together. I think Dad misinterpreted that."

"And what about Albert?" Maude asked.

"Mom looked out for him. She knew I was Dad's favorite, and she wanted Albert to feel loved."

"He called Albert a coward," I said.

"Worse names than that. Dad's a complicated man," Anise said. "I was the only person he never criticized. When he said something negative about Albert, I'd tell him to stop, but it never did much good."

"Did Albert ever do anything to justify his father's criticism?" I asked.

"No," Anise said. "Not really. They both had a bad temper, and they were both stubborn. Albert didn't want to take over the farm. He wanted a different life. He wanted to go to college, and Dad said he'd never pay for that. It upset my mother terribly that Dad would pay for a military school for Albert but not a liberal arts college. Albert couldn't breathe in that environment. Even if my mom hadn't died, I don't think Albert could have stayed at home much longer."

"And now?" I asked.

"We're family—the only family my dad has. I know Dad feels bad about how he treated Albert. Dad's a stubborn man, so he can't say that directly. But I can see how he feels when he talks to me about Albert. I thought the two of them might reconcile at my wedding, and then there was another blow-up. I don't know who started it. The only time Dad can show his soft side seems to be when he's dressed up as Santa and giving presents to the kids in Menescotta. Now, someone has taken that away from him."

"You don't think it's Albert?" Maude asked.

"No. I don't think that anymore."

"He was in the house this morning," Maude said.

"Was he looking for something?" I asked. "Snooping around for some reason?"

"Snooping?" Anise said. She laughed. "Of course you were brought here to snoop, so you assume that's what everyone else does. He's been staying here, sleeping on the couch in the master bedroom. I didn't want Dad to know, so I made up the story that he was staying with a friend. Albert comes in late and goes out early. I urged him to come. If there ever will be a real reconciliation it will happen over Christmas."

I sighed. "I don't like to say this, but Albert seems to have been around when all the damage was done, and he's an Olympic-level archer."

"Not quite that good but close. That gave Dad another opportunity to call him a loser. Albert didn't qualify at the trials."

"If he was around before you came down, where would he have stayed?" Maude asked.

"He's got some archery buddies who would have let him stay with them. We're a close community in Menescotta."

"Is there anyone in that group who might have a vendetta against your father?" Maude asked.

"Or against Christmas?" I added.

Anise turned to me. "Christmas?'

"We're just looking at all the angles. Everything that's been done seems to have focused on the holidays, making sure Bob couldn't play Santa this year. That's why I'm asking. It's possible Bob is collateral damage."

When I said it out loud, it sounded right to me. If someone wanted to kill Bob, there was plenty of opportunity to do that as Bob had pointed out. If they wanted to stop the Christmas celebration in Menescotta, then everything they did made sense. Shredding his costume, trying to let his horses out of the barn, trying to put Addy out of commission, wrecking his sleigh.

Anise shrugged her shoulders. "I've been away so long, I don't know most of the new people in Menescotta."

"It couldn't be anyone too new," I said. "It would have to be someone who knew Bob's routine, where he lived, the fact

Addy would be the horse pulling the sleigh. A newcomer wouldn't know that."

"And he wouldn't be part of the bow-and-arrow hunting club," Anise said. "That's a very elite group. It takes years to become a full member."

"Can we stop the pretense?" I asked. "There's no need for us to meet Albert in Portland when he's staying here. Can you ask Albert to meet with us sooner rather than later?"

"I can do that."

# 19

Anise stood. "I'm going to check on Dad and then the animals. I'll call Albert when I'm finished. Anything else you need from me?"

We shook our heads no. Kate entered the kitchen through the back door and the mudroom as Anise stood to leave.

"Ah, feels warm in here," she said and unwrapped her scarf.

"Too warm? Dad likes things toasty," Anise said.

"Not too warm for me," Kate said. "I've been at Wyatt's—I don't think he ever turns on the heat."

"Is there news about the sleigh?" Anise asked.

Kate looked at me, and I shook my head slightly.

"Nothing definite," Kate said.

When Anise left to go upstairs, Kate took off her coat, hung it in the mudroom and settled herself on one of the dinette chairs.

"Cup of tea available?" she asked. "Wyatt's work shed is like an ice house. He thinks he can get the sleigh ready in time for the parade. I wasn't sure what you wanted Anise to know."

"For now, I don't want anyone to know anything. Do you think Wyatt can keep his mouth shut?"

Kate shrugged. "Not sure about that. We had a nice chat while I helped him bring in pieces of the sleigh. He doesn't go out of his way to talk to anyone, but if you happen to be around, he's glad to tell you what he thinks of everyone in Menescotta."

"And?" I asked.

"I started with the people in the bow-and-arrow club, specifically the people on our list."

Kate held out her cup and Maude filled it. "Thanks." She removed her scarf. "Now, I'm getting warm again. Wyatt had a lot to say about Rudolph Samson. A nasty man is what he called him."

"Did he think he might be involved with what's been happening to Bob?"

"Wyatt said they really hated each other, and that Rudolph Samson was a man who liked to nurse a grudge, the way other people might nurse a Portland craft beer."

"What exactly does that mean?" I asked. "We know Bob scuttled his plans to sell land to Walmart and then kept him from being elected a Selectman."

"Right. What you may not know is that Samson's grudge against Bob goes back a lot further than that. Wyatt says it goes back twenty years. We know Beatrice Lohman came to work in his bank right before Ruth died. What we didn't know was that Samson hoped she might marry him eventually. He did everything he could to win her over, but he was in the midst of a messy divorce and Beatrice stayed clear. Then Bob came along, and she was all into him."

"Did Wyatt think she loved Bob," I asked, "or was she in it for the money the way everyone suspected?"

"Wyatt thought it was probably the money. He said Beatrice was savvy. She knew a messy divorce could eat up a lot of Samson's wealth. Bob was free and clear after Ruth died."

"Did Wyatt think something was going on between them before Ruth died?" I asked.

"No. He said Bob was devoted to Ruth. Actually, he said Bob was obsessed with her."

"That's the term Anise used," I said. "Did Wyatt think Samson might be after Bob now? He was in the bow-and-arrow club. Was he any good?"

"Wyatt laughed when I suggested that,' Kate said. "He didn't think Rudolph Samson could hit the side of a barn, much less an animal inside a barn. No, he didn't think Samson was directly involved. However, he did say Samson had a lot of power and money which meant he knew people who might be willing to cause trouble if he wanted them to."

"So we can't entirely rule him out," Maude said.

I filled Kate in on what we knew and what I was now thinking.

Kate nodded along as I spoke. "Your latest theory is a good one. It sounds as if this family has a lot of baggage like most families but not enough to explain what's happening to Bob now. I like your concept of collateral damage. Collateral damage means Bob could be accidentally killed, even if that wasn't what the person intended."

"He'd still be dead," Maude said, "so we have to prevent that."

"We will," I said.

I felt a swell of confidence and found myself sitting up straighter, more alert and ready for action. If the problem wasn't about Bob but about Christmas we had a new focus. If the troublemaker was a skilled archer, then the field of suspects narrowed, and if the Grinch figure had to know about Bob's routines, then it wasn't a newcomer who was set to destroy the festivities—it was someone who'd been around Menescotta for a while. Albert might be able to help with our investigation—if he showed up. He'd likely know the players.

We talked through my ideas.

"It could still be a relative newcomer who got the information he needed from others in the hunting club," Kate said.

"Possible," I said.

"How much can we tell Anise?" Maude asked. "She's not a suspect, is she?"

"No," I said, "but I'm not sure how much she'd tell Albert."

"Is Albert still a suspect?" Maude asked.

"Do you think he is?" I asked.

"No," Maude said.

"As you pointed out," Kate said, "if the goal was to kill Bob, it would be easy enough to do. He's alone on a farm. Anyone could have killed him and made it look like an accident. The motive has to be something else. And if Albert was angry with his dad, why would he wait twenty years to kill him, weeks after his sister is newly married and happy. No, I don't think Bob is the real target, and I don't think Albert is the person causing the trouble."

Anise entered the room. "Dad's fine. It will be hard to keep him in bed much longer."

She nodded when Maude offered her a cup of tea. She grabbed an unopened tin and brought out ginger snaps. "Dad's favorite. We can have a few. He'll never miss them." She sat down beside us and helped herself to a handful.

"We were going over our suspect list," I said, "and our new theory that this might be more about Christmas than your father. Maybe someone wants to scuttle the Menescotta holiday celebrations."

"Why would anyone want to do that?" she asked. "It's as big a deal as the pumpkin celebration in October."

"I came to that one year," Kate said. "All those giant decorated pumpkins and then some kind of boat race. It was hysterical." Then she stopped speaking. She sounded sad when she spoke again. "I was still with Ned at the time. He was one of the judges for the pumpkin contest."

"Ned Thompson?" Anise asked. "You know Ned? Everyone loves him."

"I can understand that," Kate said. "I think I loved him too. Is he still here in town?"

"Still judges the pumpkin contest,' Anise said. "I'm sure he'd like to see you."

Kate's face lit up. "You think so? What's he up to these days?"

"He's still a fisherman," Anise said, "still harvests alewives in the spring and then takes folks out fishing during the tourist season. Did you get to see the alewives run?"

"I did," Kate said. "It was amazing."

"Alewives?" Maude asked. "You mentioned those before, didn't you, Kate?"

"They're slender fish the lobstermen use for lobster bait," Anise said. "They're highly regulated now—almost disappeared, but this is the place to come in May. They spawn in our river and our lake."

Kate smiled and paused for just a moment. "So, Ned is doing well?"

"He's busy but never too busy for a friend," Anise said. "I'm sure he'd love to see you."

"Still single?" Kate asked.

"No," Anise said. "I'm amazed he lasted as long as he did. He married a couple of years ago. They have a young daughter, and he's a real family man. He said he was glad he waited to find the right girl—a girl who wanted the life he had to offer."

I looked at Kate. 'A girl who'd want the life he had to offer.'

Kate looked stricken and then covered her distress with a

smile. "I'm glad he's happy," she said. "He deserves to be happy."

"He does, and he is," Anise said.

Kate took a deep breath and used both hands to push herself up from the table. "I think I need to go upstairs for a bit and finish settling in."

"You look a little pale," Anise said. "Are you feeling ill?"

"Not at all. Maybe a little tired from all the driving and the chill in Wyatt's workshop."

Maude stood as if to go with her. I'm sure she saw the same thing I did—something neither of us had ever seen before. Kate looked drained of energy, drained of life.

"Thanks, Maude," Kate said, "but I can handle this. I'll take a bath and warm up and be good as new."

We watched her leave the kitchen and head upstairs. She moved the way Maude and I did when we were walking up steps—head down, hand on the handrail, moving slowly.

"Is she all right?" Anise said. "Did the news about Ned upset her? Were they a thing in the past?"

"Looks as if it was more than a thing," I said, "but whatever it was it ended years ago. We've never heard about Ned until today."

Kate didn't mention boyfriends in any detail, but we did at least know their names.

"It sounds like this is one she didn't quite get over," Maude said.

I nodded. I wondered again if Kate was re-evaluating her life and worrying she'd made mistakes along the way, big ones. I thought about her questioning me as to whether or not I was happy in my single life. I was, but that didn't mean Kate was.

We'd let Kate have her time alone, and perhaps later she'd talk to us.

I turned to Anise and moved on to the case at hand. "Is

there any chance we can get your brother to talk to us sometime today?" I asked.

"Maybe. I'll call him again. I couldn't reach him earlier, but I'll keep trying. I need to check on the animals first."

Anise left by the back door. Maude and I sat together. She offered me another cup of tea but I shook my head.

"Poor Kate," she said.

"Poor Kate," I agreed. Then, I had a most unusual thought. I wondered if I had in any way contributed to her unhappiness. "Do you think I asked too much of her? Did I keep her from finding what she wanted in life, like a meaningful relationship?"

Maude patted my hand. "She was a grown woman when she came to you. You weren't her mother. You asked things of her and she could have said no. Kate has always liked her independent life full of adventure. She may not like it now, but you are not responsible for her unhappiness."

"Thanks, Maude." I almost cried. I understood why Maude and I were such good friends. She didn't judge me. She knew how I was feeling even when I didn't know myself.

# 20

Anise returned a few minutes later. "Albert will come here. He knew someone saw him today as he was leaving, and because that person didn't call the police, he's decided he can trust you. I assured him he could. He'll bring us lunch."

"Hope it's not something he shot and killed," I said. I wasn't feeling ready for venison stew or whatever else hunters might have in their freezer.

Anise smiled. "Albert's not into hunting these days—never really was. For a while, he tried to do it to please my dad, but nothing Albert did ever seemed to please Dad."

Albert arrived an hour later with two hot pizzas and a large salad. Anise closed the kitchen door.

"I don't want the smell to bring Dad downstairs," Anise said. "I assume you want to have this discussion without him."

"Only because I thought he didn't know Albert was here," I said.

"He knows," Anise said. "He didn't for a while, but Dad recognizes every squeak and groan in this house. He heard treads on the stairs that weren't mine. That's all it took."

"Was he upset?" Maude asked.

"He didn't seem to be."

"Dad said I didn't need to keep sneaking around—the house belonged to all of us," Albert said.

I stared at him. He was a curious mixture of Bob and Anise. Same straight blondish brown hair that Anise had but with a high forehead like his father.

"You look a lot like your dad," I said.

"I'm like him in more ways than looks. That's what got us into trouble years ago. We're both stubborn with a short fuse. We're both quick to start an argument and never ready to finish it. We have trouble hearing each other. I've grown up in the last few years, but I'm not sure my dad has."

Bob entered the kitchen.

"Can't let a broken man heal, can you, Albert? I heard you bellowing from upstairs."

"Not bellowing, Dad." He helped his father sit down. "You smelled the pizza didn't you? From Pizzaro's. Got you the anchovy and cheese—I knew that's what you wanted. How's the arm?"

"Hurts," Bob said and grabbed a piece of pizza with his good hand. He waved away Anise when she tried to put salad on his plate. "No greens. Let a sick man eat what he wants."

We all helped ourselves. I avoided the anchovy pizza and settled for the olive, mushroom and pepperoni. It was delicious. After three pieces, I decided I'd had enough.

Kate joined us but said she wasn't hungry. It was a tight squeeze around that dinette table. Albert brought over two wooden chairs. There were six of us, but we made ourselves fit. Kate finally ate one piece of pizza, a good sign I thought.

To anyone looking in at us through the kitchen window, we would seem like a big, happy family.

"After all the stories I've heard," I said, "I'm surprised to see the three of you sitting around the table together."

"We wasted years being mad at each other," Anise said. "I think Dad's recent problems made us realize that."

"We've sorted a lot out in the last twenty-four hours," Albert said. "Dad needs help on the farm and Anise has a strapping husband to take care of their farm upstate. I'm moving back here—at least for a while, until Dad's on his feet."

This sounded like an enormous kumbaya moment that didn't go down as easily as the pizza. How could it be that Albert could put aside his father's disdain so easily?

"What have you sorted out if you don't mind my asking?" I said.

"The past," Albert said, "the part that matters anyway."

"You're talking about your mother's death?" I said. "Do you know what actually happened to her?"

"I do," Albert said.

Bob put down his pizza. "Albert didn't believe me at first, but I think now he does. I'm ready to clear the air for you ladies. I followed Ruth that morning. I'm ashamed to admit it, but I did. I started to have doubts about her, whether or not she still loved me, whether or not she might be thinking of leaving me for someone more handsome, someone like Charlie. Cora had the same doubts about her marriage, but I didn't know that at the time. She's always been afraid Charlie would come to mind the age difference and want a younger woman."

"So when you saw a person talking to Ruth," I said, "you thought it was Charlie because of the jacket."

"I did, but I was far away. That person, Cora it turns out, stood very close to Ruth and then suddenly turned and walked away down the path."

"She didn't touch your wife? Push her?" Maude asked.

"No, nothing like that," Bob said. "I could see Ruth staring after her, shaking her head. Then Ruth started up the path again. I nearly caught up with her when I heard her scream. I saw what she saw. A mountain lion stood on the hillside above her, crouched, looking ready to attack. I yelled at it, but I was too far away to scare it. Ruth was surprised by the sound of my voice and whirled around. That's when she lost her footing. That's when she fell."

Bob took a deep breath.

"I couldn't tell anyone at first—I felt so bad, so guilty. Maybe if I'd handled it differently, Ruth wouldn't have been startled and slipped. I finally told the police, but they didn't believe me—they said there were no mountain lions in our area. It made me a suspect in their eyes—that's one reason I don't call the police anymore when I'm in trouble. After that, I didn't tell anyone else. Not the kids, not anyone."

"Finally, Dad confessed it all to me after I kept bugging him about what happened," Albert said. "I didn't believe a word of it. Mountain lions hadn't been seen in our part of Maine for years. I thought he was making the whole thing up. Then, I began to wonder what else Dad might be hiding."

"Albert wouldn't tell me what he'd found out or what he believed," Anise said.

"Are you both convinced now that Bob is telling the truth?" I asked.

"We are," Albert said. "When Beatrice came on the scene, weeks after Mom died, that's when I really began to have doubts about the so-called accident. I began to think maybe something had been going on before Mom died. Dad was so taken with Beatrice, and she was so rotten to Anise and me. Then Dad lied about his health, and I thought he might be lying about Mom's death as well."

Bob looked at Anise. "I could see I was losing you. I couldn't bear that. That's why I made up the story about my health. I did have a cough and it worried me. The doctor said it was nothing, not like lung cancer, something really bad. That's what gave me the idea. And then it all backfired." He looked at the rest of us. "The kids found out the truth and I lost them."

"Albert and I left," Anise said. "We never discussed the morning Mom died, until yesterday. That's when I heard the truth."

"A mountain lion was spotted a few months later in the same hills," Bob said, "but by then the kids were gone. I didn't think Albert would believe me anymore than he had when I first told him about what happened."

"It's settled now, "Anise said. "We settled some of it before the wedding."

"Then, why did you send your father away after the wedding?" I asked. "Was there another argument between your dad and Albert?"

"I sent Dad away when he started to tell my husband, Caleb, how he should be farming the land. Albert took my side, and then they got into it, the way they always did."

"Dad knows nothing about growing or harvesting potatoes," Albert said.

"Not true," Bob said. "I've been farming this land for forty years, different crops but same idea."

"Caleb grew up on the farm we now own," Anise said. "You can see how stubborn Dad is, and he's always right about everything. I sent him away, so he and Caleb wouldn't get into some stupid argument that might cause bad blood between them. It was nothing more than that. We really did settle everything important before the wedding."

"Everything?" I asked. I turned to Bob. "Maybe this is none of my business, but I'm wondering why you were so hard on Albert over the years, calling him a coward and a failure."

"I regret that," Bob said. "I was a jealous man, madly in love with my wife. I could see how she favored Albert over me. She'd take his side if we had an argument. I didn't like it, so I tried to cut him down to size. I wish I could take it all back. So many years were wasted."

"You never apologized?" Maude asked.

"No, I guess I didn't. I'm not one who believes in apologizing. Water under the bridge." He turned to Albert, his face distorted in pain. "I am sorry, Albert."

To my ears, it sounded as if the apology was ripped from his gut.

"It's done now," Albert said, "and I'm tired of our arguments."

"Maybe we should move on to the current situation," Maude said. "You want to tell them your theory, Flo?"

"Anise has heard it," I said, "but I can repeat it for the rest of you. If we don't get lost in old family history, things look different. Anyone who wanted to torture or kill you, Bob, could have done it easily. You said the same thing, yourself. You're alone on the farm. It would have been simple to make your death look like a farm accident. But all the actions were directed at making sure you wouldn't be Santa in the Menescotta parade."

"Huh?" Bob said. "All of this to keep me from being Santa for the kids?"

"Maybe to stop Christmas from happening here. I mean the big public Christmas," I said. "It's almost as if whoever is doing this wanted to put his mark on his actions—using his bow and arrow to make a point—so to speak. I think that's where we start."

Bob scratched his head. "You think he wanted us to stop him?"

"I don't know about that," I said, "but all signs point to someone highly skilled in the use of a bow and arrow."

"What we need to find out," Kate said, "is if anyone in your hunt club might have a reason to hate the Christmas parade, to want to end it, to keep you from playing Santa even if you got killed in the process."

"That's a lot of hate," Anise said.

"Or a lot of hurt," Maude said. "Did anything unusual happen during the parade last year?"

"Nothing," Bob said, "not that I know of."

"You should ask Cora and Charlie about that," Anise said. "They know a lot more about what goes on in the town than Dad does."

"In the meantime, let's go over the people in the club," Kate said. "Whoever is doing this is a skilled archer, maybe a skilled woodworker as well—someone who could shave and mutilate one runner on the sleigh in a way that wouldn't be detected easily. Do you have people like that in your club?"

Bob nodded. "Everyone in the club might qualify on both counts. We currently have a membership of four men and one woman. For a while we thought the whole group would fall apart when Jackson Clark left five years ago."

"Why did he leave?" I asked.

"Don't know," Bob said. "He just told us he'd had enough. Said the whole thing was stupid and a waste of time. I always thought something personal was going on with him." He looked at Albert. "You knew Jackson growing up. Did you stay in touch with him?"

"Some," Albert said. "I heard he moved upstate, went to a lumber camp somewhere. Someone said they thought they saw him around town this winter."

"So, we have one disgruntled member to follow up on," Kate said. "Can you help us find him, Albert?"

"Sure," he said.

"Let's look at the others," I said. "I'm curious about the one woman. What can you tell us about her?"

"Fiona Dickerson," Bob said. "She hunted with us whenever she was visiting her dad. Now, she's back living here, at least for now. She's the best archer we got in the state of Maine, made the Olympic team."

"We heard all about her," Maude said.

"She made the team I didn't qualify for," Albert said. "I competed with her. She was great. We had high hopes for her, but she pulled out days before the previous summer Olympics started and I never knew why."

"Do you keep up with her?" I asked.

Albert shook his head. "But remember, I haven't been around here for years. I know she came back to Menescotta to care for her dad. He has Alzheimers I think. I imagine I could get in touch with her and see what she's been up to."

"Good," I said. "So that leaves four more people including Bob and Rudolph Samson."

"Samson may be a member," Bob said, "but he's not a hunter."

"We heard you two have a feud that dates back twenty years," I said, "over Beatrice Lohman."

"I wish I knew then what I know now," Bob said. "He could have saved me a lot of grief. He was determined to marry her, but she wanted nothing to do with him."

"Do you believe he could be the one who's doing this to you?" Maude asked.

"Could be, but he doesn't want to lose his standing in Menescotta, so I doubt it. If I caught him messing with me, the town would tar and feather him, I can promise you that. If they thought he was messing with the Christmas celebration, they'd do the same thing. And why would he? Rudolph Samson glad-hands everyone from Thanksgiving to the New Year. Even wears some silly reindeer hat and a red nose to the holiday dinners and thinks that's funny."

"How about the other two members?" I asked. "The younger ones."

"I can't see that," Bob said. "They're both eager bow-and-arrow hunters. Make their own arrows or use the ones Wyatt makes for them."

"Wyatt?" Kate asked. "He's still a member of the club?"

"Honorary at this point. At least until his eye heals. He was ticked off about that—felt like whoever did it to him, knew they'd done it and weren't owning up to it. He even accused me at one point."

"Really?" Kate asked. "Why did he think that?"

"We were hunting at dusk together when it happened. He claimed I couldn't see what I was doing."

"You don't see that well anymore, Daddy," Anise said, "especially at night."

"What—you think I nearly took out Wyatt's eye and then didn't tell him the truth about that?"

"You lied about your health," Albert said, "and you didn't tell me what happened when Mom fell until later, so we know you don't always tell the truth, especially when you feel guilty about something."

Bob was silent. For a long time. He stared at Albert.

"Can't teach an old dog new tricks," he said. "If it was me, it was an accident."

"Of course it was, Dad," Anise said, "but that doesn't mean you didn't do it."

Maude put a hand on Bob's arm. "Wishing you were perfect doesn't make you perfect, Bob. No one's perfect, and making a mistake doesn't mean you're an awful person."

Bob nodded. "I do feel guilty about Wyatt. No one else was around us. It must have been me that did it."

"Then tell him, Dad," Anise said. "All he wants is an acknowledgment and an apology. He told us his eye is going to be fine. An apology—that's all he wants, and it's all Albert wanted from you as well."

Bob nodded again and sighed. But he didn't say another word.

Time to move on.

"Do you have the arrow that landed in Addy's side?" I asked. "How is Addy doing by the way?"

"I do have the arrow and Addy's doing fine,' Bob said. "Comes home tomorrow."

"Can you identify it?" I asked.

"It's one of mine. Whoever hurt Addy stole one of my arrows first and used that."

## 21

We finished the pizza and divvied up our investigative work. That was what made Kate, Maude and me such a good team. We were methodical and thorough like most women with no grandstanding.

I commented on that to Kate.

"No grandstanding?" Kate asked. "Do you ever look in the mirror, Flo?"

"I don't know what you mean. I give credit where credit is due, and often that credit falls to me. I am, after all, the founder of ODPA, and that alone is worthy of note."

"No grandstanding," Kate said, shaking her head, eyebrows raised.

"Are you done?" I asked.

"For the moment."

We sorted through our plans one more time.

Kate was most likely to recognize the fine points of archery and the person most likely to get men to listen to her, so she would tackle the two men in the club we knew nothing about. Albert supplied the names and numbers. He offered to call them first, but Kate assured him she liked the element of surprise.

That left Jackson Clark and Fiona Dickerson.

"Maude, I think you and Albert should tackle Jackson Clark. Albert can track him down, and you can find out why he left and if he might have a grudge against Bob. Anise, perhaps you and I could talk to Fiona Dickerson. You'll give me credibility since I'm not from around here, that is if Bob can spare you."

"I can spare her," Bob said, "but why don't you let *me* help?"

"Honestly, Dad, who would open up to you if you were the one they'd injured?"

"Agreed," I said. "And if you lay low, we can spin this story however we want," I said. "We can make out you're a little more injured than you are. If the person doing this hasn't meant to harm you seriously that might get his or her attention."

"Brilliant, Flo." That was from Maude.

I held my head a little higher and smiled. "I thought so myself."

"No grandstanding, huh?" was all Kate said.

"We'll meet back here tomorrow," I said, "and see where we are."

"What about Bob," Maude asked "in case, someone wants to make sure he really is incapacitated?"

"Good point," I said. "We'll need someone discreet to keep an eye on him, take care of him as well."

"That would be Cora," Anise said, "not Charlie."

"Can those two operate separately?" I asked.

"Easily," Anise said. "Charlie isn't big on caretaking, so if we make it a mission of daily care, Charlie will stay away."

"Make sure Cora knows she's to tell no one how Bob is really doing, not even Charlie," I said. "Maybe she can say he's taken a slight turn for the worse and won't be on his feet before the new year."

"Done," Anise said.

"While you're doing that," I said, "I'll see if I can track down Fiona Dickerson."

"Her dad lives in town," Bob said. "Start there. Brayden Dickerson."

The party broke up at that point. We all had our assignments.

Maude sat beside me and pushed her laptop in my direction. "Do you need help with your computer search? I have some time while Albert is tracking down Jackson Clark."

"I've got this," I said. "Everyone seems to think I'm stuck in the 1900s. I may have been born then, but I've moved on."

Maude sat quietly beside me as I fumbled with her laptop.

"How do you make the darn thing open up?" I said.

"You need my code," she said and gave it to me. I saw the smallest smile on her lips. "Why didn't you tell me that in the first place?" I said.

"You didn't ask for it," she said, "and you hate it when people offer help you haven't asked for. Makes you feel old—that's what you've told me."

Maude smiled more broadly. "I'm good at searches. Maybe I can speed things up."

"All right." I pushed the laptop back in her direction.

"Here's an address for Brayden Dickerson," Maude said after a few seconds. "And a phone number."

I copied them both down.

"Fiona Dickerson," Maude typed. "Maine archer. Let's see what pops up when go there."

A lot popped up including a Wikipedia article about her. Those weren't always the most accurate pieces of information, but we didn't need her true life story, just a place to begin.

We sat together and read the article.

Fiona Dickerson was born in Mars Hill, Maine.

Anise joined us a few minutes later. "Cora's happy to come and stay with Bob for a day or two, so that's settled." She looked over our shoulders as we read.

"Mars Hill," she said, "that's potato country, not far from where Caleb and I live in Houlton. I heard she grew up poor and I know potato farming can be a hard life. I followed Fiona Dickerson's career but I never knew where she was born."

"When did her family move here?" I asked. "The article doesn't say much about her early life."

"Someone must have recognized her talent," Maude said. "Look, it says she trained in Portland and became a sensation before she was fifteen."

"They have that part wrong," Anise said. "I think she trained here in Menescotta, at least for a while." She paused. "I think she trained with Wyatt."

"Wyatt, the person who's repairing Bob's sleigh?" I asked.

"Yes, I think so. He was an excellent archer and also a fletcher."

"A fletcher?" Maude asked.

"A person who makes arrows," Anise responded.

"How did we not know this?" I asked.

"Unless Wyatt has changed, he doesn't give out a lot of personal information. Most Mainers don't," Anise said. "You may have noticed that."

"And we didn't know Fiona Dickerson was a person of interest at that point," Maude said, "so we wouldn't have asked him about her."

"Do you think we can trust Wyatt?" I asked.

"Absolutely," Anise said.

Wyatt had given me his cell number, so I called him. "How's the sleigh?"

"As good as new, better actually. I gave the whole thing a new coat of paint. It'll be ready in a couple of days."

"Excellent. If anyone asks you about it, tell them it's not likely to be ready for the parade."

"Someone already called me, but I did like you told me and said it was in real bad shape, might have to be scrapped."

"Good man," I said. "Who called?"

"Charlie. Surprised me. I thought he'd probably know the truth from you, but he didn't seem to, so I told him what you wanted me to. I've known Charlie his entire life. You don't think he's the one trying to hurt Bob do you?"

"Right now, we don't know what to think. I have a couple more questions, Wyatt."

"I got time. What are your questions?"

"Did you know a Fiona Dickerson?"

"Me and the rest of the world know her. Best archer in the United States of America. Damn shame what happened to her that she couldn't compete."

"What did happen?" I asked.

"I guess it can't hurt to tell you now. She got pregnant and her doc said she might lose the baby if she kept up with her Olympic training. Most people don't know what a strain archery puts on your body. She decided she couldn't take the risk. Then five months later she lost the baby anyway. Saddest thing I ever saw. Right around Christmas."

"How do you know all this?" I asked.

"We've stayed in touch. She's in town now nursing her dad. He's got dementia, and she doesn't want to put him in a home."

"We'd like to talk to her," I said.

"Fiona's a private person, especially after all she went through. Don't know if she'll feel like talking."

"Could you ask her?"

"Wanna tell me why?"

"You know what went on with the sleigh. What happened before required a talented archer."

"You've got to be kidding. You think Fiona might be involved, and you want me to let you foxes into the hen house? Nothing doing."

"I'm not accusing her of anything. Did she have any relationship with Bob?"

"You mean did she hate him and want to kill him? Sure sounds to me like you're accusing her of something."

I had the conversation on speaker phone. Maude put her hand out and took the phone.

"Hi, Mr. Miller, this is Maude."

"It's Wyatt, and you're the nice one aren't you? Bob thinks you hung the moon."

"We're just trying to get at the truth of what happened. If Fiona Dickerson is not involved, she might have an idea about who could be. She was in the bow-and-arrow hunting club for a while, wasn't she?"

"Still is as far as I know. Doesn't get down here often, but now with her dad the way he is, she'll probably be around for a few more months at least. I'll talk to her. See if she's willing to speak with you and your Old Dames Protection Agency."

"You know about us," Maude said.

"Bob told me. Cora did too. I like strong women—when they don't get too pushy."

That was undoubtedly a dig at me, but I let it pass.

I took the phone back from Maude. "Do you think we could come over tomorrow—see the sleigh and talk to Fiona if she's willing?"

"If Fiona is invited to help with your investigation, she'll be all in. But if you plan to accuse her of something, she'll curl up like a pill bug and you won't get anything out of her. I'll do the same."

"Thanks, Wyatt," I said. "What time tomorrow shall we stop by?"

"Come at eleven," he said.

We hung up, and I turned to Maude. "You'll have to handle this one."

"I'll be glad to," Maude said.

Anise popped into the kitchen, and I told her what we had planned.

"I'll come with you if that's okay," Anise said. "I've met Fiona a few times, and I'd love to talk to her again."

"Excellent," I said. "I'll try to listen more than talk."

Maude smiled.

"I will, you'll see."

"Dad's doing really well," Anise said. "He knows he can't drive the sleigh if it can be repaired, but maybe Albert or I could sit beside him and drive it."

Maude and I looked at each other. "This information is for you alone," I said. "The sleigh is good as new."

"Can I tell Dad?'

"Not yet," I said. "Don't tell anyone for now. We don't want that information slipping out."

"Deal," Anise said and left the room. "I'll tell Dad Wyatt isn't sure if he can fix it or not." We heard her quick steps heading upstairs to Bob's room.

"Now what?" Maude asked.

"Now, we wait to see what progress Albert is making in his attempt to track down our disgruntled hunter Jackson Clark."

"What do you make of Charlie's call to Wyatt?" Maude asked.

I shook my head. "I don't know what to make of it."

# 22

Maude shivered. The kitchen was warm but maybe not warm enough for her.

"Let's move to the front room and get a fire burning," I said.

Embers glowed under the andirons and there was plenty of wood and kindling in two metal containers near the fireplace. I stacked the kindling on top of the embers and built a small fire with the dried wood. I didn't even need to light a match to get things going or use what was undoubtedly an authentic nineteenth-century bellows made of beautiful carved leather.

I studied the andirons, also old and authentic. "Every item in this room is an antique," I said, "dating from the 1800s."

Maude and I settled in the two high-back chairs facing the fireplace. We were close to the front door and the central hall, so we'd hear anyone coming or going. Of course, if we could hear them, they could hear us. I stood and checked the hall to make sure no one might overhear our conversation. Then I settled back into the chair, which was remarkably comfortable for being close to two hundred years old.

"This is a special room," Maude said. "I could spend all

day here. It's like being in a museum— a living one. I suspect Ruth was a special person. She created this room, and Bob maintained it. I think they really loved each other. It's sad Bob didn't trust her in the end."

"Anise made it sound as if he was obsessed with her, and Bob admitted he was a jealous man."

"What a shame," Maude said. "I was too trusting of my own husband, and Bob wasn't trusting enough of Ruth. I wonder if the same could be said about Cora. Does she really have something to worry about with Charlie or is it all in her head?"

"I can't make sense of the relationship between Cora and Charlie," I said. "I know they've been together for years, and it was Cora's mother who emailed you for help. Cora wouldn't have allowed that if she thought Charlie might have been involved in what was happening to Bob. But why would Charlie call Wyatt to see about the sleigh?"

"I suppose," Maude said, "he might have called out of concern for Bob and the parade."

"Then why didn't he simply believe what we told him?"

Maude raised both hands, palms open, and made a face. "Mystery to me. I don't know much about Charlie. Ida said her daughter kept him a secret from everyone. She thought it was because Cora was older than he was and embarrassed about that fact."

"He's ten years older?"

Maude nodded.

"So she's a cougar," I said. "Ten years doesn't seem like that much. She'll probably outlive him anyway."

Maude sighed. "It's fine for men to be decades older than the women they marry, but ten years is considered a lot if the woman is older. Cora certainly seems bothered by it."

"The irony is that Cora looks as young as Charlie, maybe younger," I said. "If someone ought to be worried, it's Charlie.

Cora is a handsome woman, but, of course, that's not the way the world works."

"Cora jokes about Charlie's appreciation of other women," Maude said, "but I'm not sure she really thinks it's funny. It wouldn't be funny to me."

"It broke up your marriage, Maude, so I can understand that. I, for one, never liked a man with a wandering eye."

"I don't think Cora does either," Maude said. "She keeps denying it's a problem, but I wonder if she really feels that way."

"Any chance you could check that out?"

'Before or after we talk to Fiona and Wyatt?" Maude asked.

"That happens tomorrow," I said. "Maybe you could talk to Cora today. Maybe Anise and I could dream up an excuse to talk to Charlie about something else."

Anise entered the room. "I heard my name mentioned. What are you two planning?"

I went over my questions.

"This town loves Charlie," Anise said, "you should know that. He's always ready with a helping hand. He's big into every festival we have. And if someone is in trouble, Charlie and Cora are first on the scene."

"Is it the women who love him," I asked, "or is it really everyone?"

Anise thought for a moment. "There's never been a scandal about him if that's what you're wondering. I would have heard from one of my girlfriends even after I left town. He is kind of a flirt, so he might be more popular with the women than the men. But I think Cora's right when she says he looks but doesn't touch. I would have heard otherwise."

"Why would he go behind our backs and check on the sleigh?" I asked. "He called Wyatt directly to find out how repairs were coming, and Wyatt said what we told him to say—that the sleigh might have to be scrapped."

"Charlie does what he wants when he wants," Anise said, "and he's almost like a woman in the way he loves gossip." She stopped. "Did I just insult womenkind?'

"A lot of women I know do love to gossip," I said. "I don't happen to be one of them. Why don't you call Cora for a visit, maybe a little Christmas shopping in town this afternoon, before she settles in to keep an eye on Bob? Maude and I will try to talk to Charlie while you're gone."

"Sure," Anise said. "I'd like to find something for Caleb. This was going to be our first Christmas together after our marriage."

"I'm sorry about that," Maude said.

"It's all right. He understands, and he'll be here Christmas Day. Still, I'd like to get him a special gift." She lifted one hand in the air as if she'd had a thought. "While we're shopping, I can find out what some of the shopkeepers know about Bob's predicament. I can see if anyone has a theory about who might be behind the mischief."

"Excellent," I said.

Once again we had our assignments, and that always made me happy.

Albert and Kate turned up as we were putting on our coats and boots.

"Did you find the other men in the hunting group?" I asked.

"Both accounted for and both with alibis, it seems," Kate said, "visiting relatives or home with their families on the night Bob was wounded."

"I let the word get around that he wasn't likely to make it to the parade," Albert said. "I said he wasn't in good shape with a sleigh that might be beyond repair. I also tracked down Jackson Clark. He's staying with friends in town."

"Do you think he'll talk to us?"

"Don't know, but I'll check."

"Thanks, Albert," I said.

Kate and I tromped upstairs to check on Bob and found him seated near the window, looking out on his backyard and barn. The snow was turning a muddy brown, the way it did after some time without new snow. The trees were bare, but the barn still had a layer of snow on its roof.

"I need to get out of here," he said, "check on the animals and clean up things. Get rid of any ice dams that might be forming on the roof."

"You won't be much use with one good arm," Kate said. "You certainly can't get on the roof and shovel snow. Anise and Albert will do what needs doing."

"Be patient for a few more days, please," I said. "We want people to imagine you're resting up, not quite yourself. Cora is coming to stay with you for a couple of days to make it look like you need care."

"You gonna ask Wyatt about the sleigh?" Bob asked.

"We plan to talk to Wyatt and Fiona tomorrow, so we'll check on the sleigh," I said.

"Tell him thanks and that I need to talk to him," Bob said.

"If it's about an apology," Maude said, "I think you should initiate that yourself—you have his phone number, don't you?"

"I do." He looked at Maude. "You can read me like a book. I guess you're trying to tell me to take responsibility for what I do, be a man. My Ruth tried to tell me that on more than one occasion."

Maude smiled at him, and he smiled back—a warm, gooey smile.

"I don't mean to intrude on this love fest," I said, but of course that was precisely what I meant to do. "We need to get back to work—we'll drive over to Wyatt's place tomorrow."

"Can I come?" Kate asked.

She sounded like a small child.

"Fiona Dickerson is probably the best archer in the world," Kate said. "Certainly, the best in the US. I'd love to meet her."

"As long as we have someone guarding Bob, that will work."

Next stop was Cora and Charlie. We decided on a surprise visit. Kate drove us there. We hadn't intended to spy on them, but in the end that's what happened.

# 23

Charlie and Cora's drive hadn't been plowed after the recent snow, so we parked off the main road and walked through the snow to the front door. The air was still and the house was picture perfect, snow drifting off the eaves with the Christmas wreath on the front door. What we heard as we climbed the front steps was less picturesque.

Cora was shouting.

"Charlie, you always do this. Some stranger asks you for help and you're off running. I ask for help and you say you'll do it tomorrow. You said you'd plow the drive, not done. You said you'd drive me to town, not done. Maybe this stranger isn't a stranger at all. Female, I'll bet, and attractive."

Maude started to ring the bell, but I put my hand up to wait a bit. I wanted to hear Charlie's response. Instead, I heard a clump of boots headed down the hall to the door.

"Now," I mouthed, vigorously nodding my head.

Maude rang the bell one second before Charlie opened the door. As soon as he saw us, his face transformed. His narrowed eyes opened wide. His lips set in a thin line turned into a grin, and he stopped in his tracks.

"Hope you haven't been here long," he said.

"No," I lied. "I apologize for not calling first."

"No worries," he said. He yelled back to Cora. "We have visitors."

Cora joined Charlie at the door. She wasn't as good at disguising her emotions as Charlie was. She looked embarrassed. "I hope you didn't hear the discussion Charlie and I were having. We tend to be loud at times."

I found it harder to lie to Cora, so I said nothing.

"Looks like you had to walk up in the snow," Cora said. "I was telling Charlie we needed to get the drive plowed. Come in."

"I was about to work on that," Charlie said. "You need me for anything in here?"

Cora shook her head.

"You have your own snowplow?" Kate asked.

"Most folks do," Charlie said. "We help out those who don't. That's why I haven't gotten to our drive yet. I'll do it now."

"Mind if I come with you?" Kate asked. "It sounds silly, but I've never ridden on a snowplow, and it might be fun."

"Sure," Charlie said.

Change in plans. If we wanted to know how much of a player Charlie really was, Kate might find that out. A lot of men found her irresistible with her toned body, olive complexion and jet black hair.

"Take your time," I said. "We'll visit with Cora—if you have time for that, Cora."

"I do," she said, "and I'd love it."

Kate headed out with Charlie.

"Let me help you out of your things," Cora said. "Then we can sit by the fire and chat. I'd love the company, and I'd love to hear how the investigation is going."

Cora gathered our coats and hung them on the coat rack.

"I always have a fresh supply of clean warm socks if you want to take off your boots.

We did. That seemed to be the custom here. Maude and I examined the basket of socks Cora offered us.

"These look home knit," Maude said, "with non-skid backings on the bottom."

"I have a lot of time on my hands, especially in winter."

We each picked a pair and sat on the bench in the hallway to put them on.

"Beautiful bench," I said, "hand carved?"

"Yes. Charlie's a wonderful woodworker when he puts his mind to it, which isn't as often as I'd like."

She sighed.

"It's none of our business," I said, "but are you and Charlie doing all right?"

Cora looked startled by my remark, and then she looked angry. "I don't want you to start dissecting my relationship with Charlie, Flo. You did that once to my mother and nearly broke her heart. I know it was a long time ago, and I realize it was for the best, but you really hurt her."

"I'm sorry about that," I said, although I didn't mean it. "I couldn't see any way to convince her that the man she was thinking of marrying wasn't any good. I thought the only way she'd recognize the truth was to see it with her own eyes. Lucky for you, I'd say. Otherwise you'd have ended up with a scoundrel for a father."

"I know you were right to do it, but the whole thing was so humiliating for her. She was young and naive and full of hope. She said he was the first man she'd ever loved. It made it difficult for her to trust men again, and she passed that mistrust on to me."

"You don't trust Charlie?" The words were out of my mouth before I could take them back.

Cora stood and wrung her hands. "Don't do this, Flo. I can't bear it."

Maude touched Cora's arm. "Sit down, dear. Flo means no harm, but she's still her outspoken self. We heard the argument —that's what started all this."

"It was just that," Cora said, "an argument, an old one, the kind married people have every day. You never married, Flo, so I don't think you know about the give and take of relationships. But you were married, Maude."

"I'm afraid I'm not the best example of a happily married woman," Maude said. "You might say Flo and I are both jaded. Is yours a happy marriage?"

"Happy enough," Cora said. She sat down across from us, her back to the fire. "We agree on most things—how to raise children, how to work the farm. I've always been the one more content with a simple life. I'm not sure Charlie ever got the wanderlust out of his system, and he doesn't like anyone telling him what to do or butting into his business. When I asked you to come investigate what was going on with Bob, Charlie went berserk."

"Do you know why?" I asked.

"He said outsiders—especially outsiders from a big city like Boston— had no place investigating problems in Menescotta. The local police could follow up on any difficulties Bob was having."

"Charlie didn't show us he felt that way," Maude said. "He was warm and welcoming."

"That's Charlie," Cora said. "He's very good at being pleasant to people. Everyone thinks he's the sweetest guy in the world, but he's got a temper. You heard it."

"Actually, we only heard your voice," I said.

Cora nodded. "I have a temper, too."

Maude spoke up. "If you don't want another word said

about Charlie, we'll stop, but if you're willing, we'd like to ask a few more questions."

"About Charlie?" Cora sighed deeply. "My mother invited you here to investigate, Maude. We knew we could trust you, and Mom said Flo was honest to a fault. Ask whatever questions you need to ask."

"Thank you," I said, but this was Maude's ballgame, and I needed to keep my mouth shut.

"I think we want to know a little more about Charlie," Maude said. "I've never met him before. You've been married a long time, so you must know him very well. I can tell you love him."

"I do love him. Sometimes, I think I love him too much. The kids kept us glued together for most of our married life, but they're off on their own now. It's just the two of us, and I wonder if I'm enough for Charlie. I'm ten years older than he is. It didn't matter when we married, but I wonder if it matters now."

"Why do you say that?" Maude asked.

"Charlie's a good-looking man, even at fifty-two. Men get more attractive as they age while women . . . become invisible."

"I don't feel the least bit invisible," I said.

Maude ignored me. "I know what you mean, Cora. People ignore me or take me for a pathetic old woman who needs help to walk or sit down. It's only my money that makes them pay attention to me."

"And your mind," I said.

"Most men don't care much about a woman's mind, Flo," Maude said. "Why do you believe Charlie might be unhappy with his life, Cora?"

"He's always away lately. I wonder if he's imagining what life might be like with a younger woman."

"What makes you think that?" Maude asked.

"Oh, Maude, you've seen how he looks at women," she said.

"If he isn't careful, people will think he's a dirty old man," I said.

"Really, Flo, that's enough." This was from Maude.

"Hear me out," I said. "The point I'm trying to make is that Charlie doesn't look younger than you, Cora. You look amazing, and Charlie—well, to be honest—Charlie's gone a little bit to pot."

Cora smiled. "I'd think you're being kind, but my mother assured me you never say things simply to make someone else feel better."

I wondered if I should be insulted by that remark and decided it wasn't worth the effort.

"I've always thought Charlie simply liked to look," Cora said. "I mean, I can admire a handsome man even at my age. But lately, he spends more and more time away from the house, and I don't know what he's up to."

"When did that change occur?" I asked.

"You know, it happened right after I called you and you agreed to come. I hadn't thought about the timing before. I knew he wasn't pleased I called, but after that he was gone at all hours."

"That's odd," I said. "He didn't explain where he was?"

"He didn't even try to explain beyond saying he had friends who needed his help. Bob was one of them. I knew how upset Bob was about his costume being shredded, so I was fine if Charlie wanted to spend time with him. But when I asked Bob about Charlie's visits, he said he hadn't seem much of him."

"Do you have any idea where he might have gone?" Maude asked.

"None. Sometimes he'd be gone late at night, so I don't know."

Maude asked the question I was dying for her to ask.

"We need to ask you this, and it might upset you," Maude said.

"You want to know where Charlie was in the early morning when Bob saw a man with a gun and an arrow scratched his face." Cora suddenly seemed short of breath. "I don't know. He wasn't home."

"Oh," Maude said.

I realized something as Cora told the story. At least two people had to be involved that night, assuming Bob was honest about what he saw. One person opened the barn door, and another person shot an arrow from the opposite direction and from a height—all in the dark of the early morning. I kept those thoughts to myself.

"Charlie could never harm Bob," Cora said.

"And yet there was a time years ago when Bob thought Charlie might be making a play for his wife," I said, "and Bob suggested you had the same worries."

"It was a bad time for the four of us. Then Ruth died before anything got resolved, but that was twenty years ago."

"You think now that nothing was going on?" Maude asked.

"That's what I think. I don't know for sure, but it's old history, and when I accused Ruth, she got so upset. I still feel bad about that."

I wondered if we'd gotten all we could from Cora, and I could see Maude felt the same way. She changed the subject.

"The house looks lovely, Cora. Ready for a big Christmas. Will your kids be coming home?"

"Not this year. I cheer myself up by decorating. It can be terribly lonely here in the winter, and that might be another reason I let Mother invite you here. You were always like a second mother to me, Maude, and I wanted your warmth."

"I'm glad I'm here then," Maude said.

I got up and padded down the hall. Perhaps they needed a

little time together. I didn't get far before Charlie and Kate opened the front door.

"Stand back, Flo," Kate said. "It's cold out here. We had the best time. Who knew riding on a snowplow could be so much fun?"

Charlie smiled. "It *was* fun. We almost landed in a ditch but Kate saved the day."

I helped Kate out of her coat. "Much to tell," she whispered.

# 24

Charlie stomped his feet on the outside mat and again on the one inside. He didn't remove his coat. "I've got other people who need to be plowed out. Could take a while."

"Cora, we'll take you over to Bob's," I said, "Charlie can pick you up there or we can drop you back here. Kate's an expert driver in the elements."

Charlie nodded. "She is. I let her drive for a while. She's a natural."

"Maybe you could spend the night if Charlie doesn't mind?" I said. "It would make it easier to look after Bob."

"I'd like that."

"Fine with me," Charlie said.

Cora gave him a peck on the cheek and left to get some things together.

"Well, ladies, I'm off," Charlie said.

Kate, Maude and I settled ourselves in the front room.

"Quickly, what happened?" I asked Kate.

"If you mean, did he make a pass at me?" Kate said. "He absolutely did not. He was kind and interested in my life. He asked about boyfriends but not in a creepy way. Either I'm not his type or Charlie isn't a man who fools around."

"I'm glad to hear that," I said. "Of course, if Charlie is the least bit smart, he'd know he shouldn't fool around with a member of ODPA, even an honorary member."

"I don't get that vibe from him," Kate said, "but I suppose I could be wrong."

"Or maybe Cora is," I said.

"Cora is what?" Cora asked entering the room with a small overnight bag.

"I mentioned that I hoped you'd bring some Christmas cheer to a house that seems pretty glum at the moment."

"Bob's house? Yes, I'm sure it's glum, particularly if it looks like he's out of the parade. I know where Ruth kept her Christmas decorations. I'm sure Bob hasn't thrown them away. We'll pull them out if he lets us."

We did just that. Bob was asleep when we arrived, but Anise thought it was a wonderful idea. In two hours the house glowed with Christmas spirit. Apparently Ruth had a thing for Santas in all shapes and sizes along with scented candles. We put them everywhere. Cora made hot cider with cinnamon and cloves. Anise brought in armloads of greenery and a small Christmas tree—chopped from Bob's property.

"He'll never miss it," she said.

We were busy decorating the tree when Bob hobbled downstairs.

"It looks as if you hurt your leg in the fall," Anise said, "as well as your arm. Did you?"

"Nope. Just arthritis." He looked at the hallway and then in the family room. "What have you done?"

He didn't sound exactly pleased.

"We are brightening up your world, Bob," I said.

"I hope you don't mind," Maude said. "Cora's going to stay overnight, and we thought we might have our own early Christmas celebration here."

"It doesn't change what's going to happen next week, or not going to happen," Bob said.

Maude put a hand on his arm. "It will all work out."

I had a sudden inspiration.

"What if you have an open house next week after the parade?" I asked. "You can dress in your new Santa outfit and pass out presents with your good arm."

"Your house is big enough," Cora said. "We'll handle refreshments."

"It's a wonderful idea," Maude said. "The children can sit on your lap—that's not something they get to do in the parade."

"If you say it's a wonderful idea, Maude," Bob said, "then I guess I can go along with that."

Good grief. Bob, with his Maude crush, was as subtle as a sledge hammer.

"And maybe," I said, "the sleigh will be fixed by next week. Perhaps Anise could drive it for you as one of your elves."

"Lots to hope for," Maude said.

"Lots," Bob responded, giving her a dewy-eyed look.

Did Maude not see what she was doing? Had she been out of the man market so long, she didn't realize when one was flirting with her? Or when she was flirting back? I needed to have a long chat with her.

Cora brought in mugs of hot cider. We sat around the fire drinking the cider and sharing old Christmas stories. Ours were mostly about saving someone from harm over the holiday season, but Cora's and Bob's were more about the town. Most were happy memories but not all.

"Like you," Cora said, "we had some rough patches over

Christmas, but unlike you, we couldn't always save people from harm. I guess you know the story about Fiona Dickerson. First, she had to pull out of the Olympics to save her pregnancy, and then the baby died anyway right around Christmas. That was a terrible tragedy."

"Was she married?" I asked.

"Engaged," Cora said, "and that was another blow. The tragedy ended her engagement. Jackson couldn't handle it, and Fiona moved away."

"Jackson? As in Jackson Clark?" I asked.

Cora nodded.

"They were engaged?"

"It was a very quiet engagement. I think Fiona didn't want anyone to know before the Olympics. And she certainly had no plans to get pregnant. That's what she told our daughter, and then she swore her to secrecy, so that wasn't how I heard about it. Only the people in the hunting club knew anything about it."

"I was the one who told you," Bob said.

"I think you were. Charlie never said a word, which surprised me. He usually can't keep his mouth shut when it comes to gossip, but in this case he did."

Two people entered the room as we finished our cider—Albert and a man I didn't know.

"What's this?" Albert asked. "This place looks the way the house looked when Mom was alive. We could see the decorations through the front window."

He took off his coat and hung it on a hall tree beside the front door. The other man made no move to remove his coat.

This is Jackson Clark," Albert said.

We made the introductions. Jackson looked as if he'd been dragged into the house kicking and screaming. If he hadn't been scowling, he would have been a handsome man. He was tall, about Albert's height with the same hair coloring, sandy blond. Unlike Albert's round face, Jackson's was craggy, his mouth twisted into what might be a chronic frown.

"I'm not happy to be here," he said. "No offense but I've got work to do."

"What work would that be?" I asked.

"I'm a logger. Off season, I'm a general handyman. Things break down in winter, so I'm getting lots of calls and work's backing up."

"I thought you didn't live in Menescotta anymore." I said.

"I don't, but this year it seemed like I might want to be here again."

"Is that because Fiona Dickerson is here nursing her dad?" I asked.

Jackson took a step toward me, and I could see the muscles in his arms flex.

"What's that got to do with anything?" Jackson said. He looked at me. "Albert said you were a nosy busybody, but that I'd do better talking to you than trying to avoid you. So, I'm here talking to you. What does any of this have to do with Fiona?"

"If you're talking about Bob's troubles, we're not sure," I said, "but, we found out you were engaged to Fiona when she lost her baby. Your baby, I'm assuming. When was that?"

Jackson took another step toward me, and Albert stopped him. "Cool off," he said.

"Course it was my baby," Jackson said. "What are you implying?'

"She's not implying anything," Maude said. "Why don't you sit down by the fire, and I'll get you some cider."

"I don't want cider. I don't want to sit down. I don't want to be here."

"Easy does it," Bob said. "Maude is offering you hospitality. Take it."

"Maude, is it?" Jackson said. "You on a first-name basis with these old birds who claim to be detectives?"

That seemed to rouse everyone. Kate stood in front of Jackson before Bob could get to him. "I'm one of those 'old birds' and I'm pretty sure you don't want to mess with me."

"Or me," Albert said. "Sit down and chill out. Tell them what they want to know and you can get out of here."

Jackson looked around the room like a trapped moose. He was a big man, and he could have wreaked havoc in the overly decorated room but he chose not to.

He sat.

Cora brought him a mug of cider, and he drank it.

"Now," I said, "about Fiona. Is that why you're back in town?"

"So what if it is?"

"How long has it been since you've seen her?" Maude asked.

"Since the baby died," Jackson said, "five years."

"Fives years is a long time," Maude said.

"She wouldn't see me before now."

"What changed?" Maude asked again. She shifted places with me, so she could sit a little closer to Jackson—not too close, but close enough so she wouldn't have to raise her voice to work her magic.

"I think it was her dad," Jackson said. "When it was clear he was losing his memory and couldn't cope, Fiona knew she needed to come home. And I think she started to realize how short life was, too short for old feuds. She tracked me down somehow and called me! That took my breath away. I thought she'd never forgive me for how I acted, but she said she had."

"How you acted?" I asked.

Jackson seemed to think it was Maude who'd asked the question.

"I couldn't handle it," Jackson said. "When the baby died

right after it was born, I couldn't bear to look at it or hold it. I couldn't bear to see how miserable Fiona was. So I left. I left her in the hospital. Got drunk and high. I planned to go back and apologize but staying high was easier."

Jackson took a last sip of cider and then clutched the mug with both hands. "I didn't even know where I was or what I was doing for a month. When I finally came to my senses, Fiona was gone.

"Her dad wouldn't have anything to do with me. Who could blame him? He refused to tell me where she'd gone—just told me to leave her alone. That's when I left the hunting club and everyone I knew here. I could tell people were disgusted with me. Bob and Charlie most of all. They were family men, and they couldn't understand my behavior. I couldn't understand it myself. I left Menescotta and went to logging camps. A lot of us were misfits in those camps, so I felt like I belonged there. When I got tired of one group of guys I'd find another camp—Maine, Canada, didn't matter to me."

Jackson handed the mug to Cora who was standing beside him. "Then, out of the blue, Fiona called me. I don't know how she found me. She said it was time we talk."

"Are you two back together now?" Maude asked.

Jackson shrugged. "I don't know." He rubbed a hand over his face and over his unkempt hair. "She told me she wasn't ready to see me yet and that I had to be patient. I could hear the suffering in her voice even over the phone. It was Christmas time, her dad so ill. I knew she'd be thinking about the baby we'd lost, and I promised her I wouldn't run away from her ever again.

"Then I saw Bob, all cheerful with plans to play Santa for the season, and something snapped. I couldn't let Fiona go through another miserable Christmas in Menescotta—not with everyone around her full of smiles and good cheer. Nope, not going to happen!"

"You know, not everyone loves Christmas," Maude said. "I sometimes didn't until I met Flo."

"I don't care about anyone else. When Fiona and I were suffering before, I ran away. This time I wasn't going to do that."

"So you took out your pain on Bob," I said. "You were behind everything that's been happening to him."

Jackson stood and paced. He started for the front door but stopped when Maude called out to him.

She patted the seat beside her. "We just want to hear your side of the story, Jackson."

He sat down again and glared at Bob. "Bob can be so smug —like he has all the answers. When Fiona lost the baby, he was in the hospital in his Santa suit giving away presents. What present could he give us? Could he bring our baby back to life? Instead, he talked about losing his wife and how he got over it."

Jackson stared at Bob. "It wasn't the same thing. Losing a baby isn't the same thing."

Bob nodded. "You're right."

"All I wanted to do," Jackson said, "was to stop all those smug faces from enjoying a Christmas this year that Fiona and I would never enjoy."

"You didn't care if you killed Bob in the process?" I asked.

"I was never going to kill him. I only wanted to shut down the parade. I didn't want Fiona to suffer through another Christmas in Menescotta that would remind her of all she'd lost."

"You very nearly did kill him," I said. "Who was with you that night at the barn?"

"What are you talking about?" Jackson asked. "No one was with me."

"Bob saw you with a gun and then an arrow nearly took off his head," I said.

"What? That wasn't a gun. It was a wrench to break the

lock if I needed to, but Bob hadn't locked his barn doors. I heard him shout at me and then I saw him hit the ground. I didn't know what had happened."

Anise said she needed to make a phone call and left the room.

I kept asking questions, and Jackson kept answering them.

"I know nothing about the arrow that could have killed Bob. I admit I cut up the costume—that was easy to do when Bob was in town. I thought that would be the end of it. Then Anise shows up with a new costume. I thought—no horse, no Santa on a sleigh. It wasn't hard to cause a slight wound to the younger horse. The old one wouldn't be fit to pull a sleigh. I whittled down one runner on the sleigh just in case. I knew Bob always took his sleigh out for a test run, and I was there when he tried it out with his old horse Bessie. I stayed around to make sure nothing terrible happened. I saw the sleigh tip and fall. Bessie got away, but Bob didn't. Before I could get to Bob, you all ran up."

Anise re-entered the room. "I called Fiona. Wyatt gave me her number. She's on her way."

# 25

"Fiona's coming here?" Jackson said.

He grinned and his whole image transformed. He went from menacing to adorable. There was no other word for it. I looked at Maude and she nodded.

"Now, I can see why someone might fall in love with him," she whispered to me. "He looks like a little kid himself, and he has to be thirty at least."

He walked to the mirror above the fireplace and tried to slick back his hair. "You got a bathroom downstairs?'

Anise pointed down the hallway. "You look fine, Jackson."

"Want to wash my hands, my face. This isn't how I intended to see Fiona for the first time in five years. Does she know I'm here?'

"She does," Anise said. "That's partly why she's coming. She said it was time."

"Time to see me again?" Jackson asked.

"She didn't specify what it was time for, but when she heard that we were sorting through what had happened to Bob, she said she needed to come."

Jackson disappeared down the hall.

"He doesn't seem to know someone was there with him the night he tried to take the horses away," Maude said.

"Do you think he's lying about that?" Cora asked. "Do you think it could have been Charlie?" She looked shaken.

"What are you talking about, Cora?" Bob said. "You think Charlie took a shot at me in the dark? I don't believe it. Why would he do that?"

Cora shook her head. "I don't know what Charlie's been up to lately. I never see him."

"We're jumping to conclusions," I said. "Let's see what Fiona has to say. If we have to, we'll drag Charlie in here for an explanation of where he was that night. For now, we wait on Fiona."

Jackson returned and paced the floor.

"Jackson," I said, "a waitress at the River Lodge restaurant in Menescotta thought she saw a young man talking to Rudolph Samson. We thought it was Albert, but you two have the same coloring. Was it you?"

"I don't know what you're talking about. If I was ever that close to Rudolph Samson I would have slugged him, not talk to him. He forced my parents out of their home when they couldn't pay the mortgage."

"Whoever it was sounded as if they were threatening Bob," I said. "Samson apparently said, 'We need to teach that old man a lesson,' and the other person said, 'A permanent one.' "

Kate looked at me and smiled. "You remember that word for word—you've still got it, Flo."

"So who was that?" I asked.

"It was me," Albert said without any hesitation. "We do have more than one old man in town, Flo. I don't like Samson much, but he offered me a job. And I need a job to stay here. He was unhappy with his bank teller and wanted him out. He thought he might be skimming money off the till but couldn't prove it. That's what the conversation was all about."

"Hmm" I said. "You know we can check that easily."

"I know. Check away."

Anise stood next to Albert. "You really are going to stay?"

"Yes. I need steady work, so I can help Dad. I suppose you don't think much of my new job, Dad, do you? Not a real man's job in your mind."

Bob shook his head. "I'm working on being a better man, Albert. A job like that will let you help me on the farm. And it will give you the time you need to go to college if you still want to do that. I know how much you love your books, and I suspect that hasn't changed. Anise can sell some land to Charlie and get you the money you need for school."

Maude took Bob's hand. "You're a good man, Bob."

Oh, no. I half expected Bob to grab Maude and give her a smack on the lips. I was relieved when he didn't do that.

"You are so like Ruth and my mother," he said. "Did you know my mother's name was Maude? She was a woman just like you—warm, caring and strong. It's what my Ruth would have become if she'd lived long enough, a matriarch with a warm heart—unlike what happens to some powerful women when they age."

Bob looked at me as he spoke, and he must have seen the expression on my face.

"I'm not talking about you, Flo," he said. "You are also a matriarch with a heart. You simply do a better job of keeping that heart under wraps than Maude does."

He smiled at me, and I did my best to smile back.

"Secret's out," Kate said.

We heard the sound of a truck approaching and watched Jackson run out to the porch. I commented on the fact that it was a little stuffy in the room and opened the front window. From there I could see and hear most of what was happening outside.

"Really, Flo, can't you give them some privacy?" Kate asked.

"No. I need to see how they deal with each other initially."

"Hmm," was all Kate said, but she stood beside me.

Fiona climbed out of the truck—Wyatt's truck. She looked lovely, even in her coat and boots. Her cheeks were pink and her face was devoid of make-up. She was thirty if I remembered correctly, but she looked more like an eighteen-year-old. She removed her cap and shook out her dark hair. Slowly, she approached Jackson. Neither one of them spoke.

Jackson came down the porch steps and waited. When she was five feet away, Fiona put out her hand. Jackson walked up to her and shook it. He seemed to have trouble letting go.

"You look exactly the same," he said. "I am so sorry. The worst thing I ever did in my life was to leave you when you needed me."

"No," Fiona said, withdrawing her hand. "The worst thing you ever did in your life was trying to hurt Bob simply because he wanted to celebrate Christmas in the town I love. When I heard what was happening I knew it had to be you. I followed you that early morning you went to Bob's and opened the barn doors. I was afraid one of you would kill the other. All I had with me was my bow and arrow and a set of car keys. I rattled them as loud as I could. I thought in the still air you might hear them and look up and see me on the roof. But you didn't. I was scared Bob might shoot you as an intruder, so I fired a warning shot, near enough to Bob to force him to duck."

She folded her arms across her chest. "I really thought maybe you'd changed in five years. I knew I had, but you're just as hot-headed as ever."

Jackson stepped back and put his head down. "I couldn't bear your suffering," he said.

"You couldn't bear your own suffering—the way you couldn't bear it five years ago. You never asked me if I was still in pain. I'm not, Jackson. I've moved on and I thought maybe you had too. It seems I was wrong."

Time to intervene. I walked to the door and opened it wide. "Could you two come inside, so you don't freeze to death out there?"

Fiona looked up at me. "You must be Flo," she said. "Wyatt described you perfectly. He called you a formidable creature who always spoke her mind. I'm so glad to meet you."

She entered the house, and Jackson followed behind. I led them both to the main room. Bob got out of his chair with difficulty. "I heard you were back in town," he said. "I'm glad to see you. I've been meaning to see your dad."

"If you're serious about that, you should do it soon," Fiona said. "He may not recognize you, but he'll still enjoy your visit."

Maude and Anise got everyone seated. Kate remained standing with her back to the fire. She looked awe-struck. "You're my hero," she said.

Fiona smiled. "It's nice to hear you say that. I let a lot of people down, I know."

"If you mean about the Olympics, you did what you had to do," Kate said. "I'm sorry it didn't work out the way it should have."

Fiona nodded. "It took me a long time to come to terms with all of it, but I have now. I'm in a better place. I was on the Olympic training staff this time around."

"I never saw your name mentioned," Kate said.

"I wanted to keep a low profile, but I'm proud of my girls, very proud. In the next Olympics we'll bring home some medals."

Maude and Cora offered more cider to anyone who was interested, along with homemade cookies.

"Time to talk," I said. "You hurried over here as if you had something to tell us."

Fiona looked at me. "I suspect you heard most of it when you were listening at the open window."

I had the decency to blush. "I'm not sure everyone else did. Can you tell us what's been going on from the beginning?"

Fiona nodded. "I needed to come home to take care of my father. I knew it was time to make peace with my past. I contacted Jackson before I came to see if we might talk through what happened five years ago. He said he was ready. I wanted to have that conversation on the phone once I was back in town. I told him I would see him when I was ready, and he agreed to that."

"I kept my word about that," Jackson said.

"You did, but I could tell how upset you were about everything—even over the phone. You're still angry. I don't know who you're angry at, but I could see you hadn't moved on. That really disappointed me. You kept talking about making amends, how you'd make it all up to me, so I'd never have to suffer again."

Jackson nodded. "It was unbearable to hear the sadness in your voice."

"Of course, I'm sad, Jackson. My father is dying and he barely knows me. Some days are better than others, and I celebrate those days."

"I thought it was about the baby, the town where everything went wrong at Christmas."

"You should have asked me, Jackson. I would have told you I'm okay. It doesn't sadden me to see children enjoying Christmas. It brings me joy. And hope."

"I didn't know," Jackson said. "I only wanted to spare you pain."

"You can't do that for another person. You can't take away their pain, but you can stick around, stay by their side."

"I screwed up again," Jackson said, "badly."

"You did," Fiona responded. "I had to dig you out of the

hole you were digging for yourself. And I needed help to do that. That's where Charlie came in."

"Charlie?" Cora asked. "My Charlie?"

Fiona smiled. "Your Charlie. We decided the two of us could see what Jackson was up to and keep Bob safe."

"Charlie tried to talk to me," Jackson said, "and I told him to mind his own business. I told him he didn't know what he was talking about—he didn't know a thing about grief."

"I tried to talk to you, too," Fiona said, "and you wouldn't listen to me either. I know about grief. I know you can't run from it or pretend everything is all right. Time with my dad has taught me that. Our time now is bittersweet, but it's precious. Even the seconds when our little girl was alive are precious to me. You've missed out on so much, Jackson, by being bitter and afraid. I'm sorry for you."

"Is it hopeless for us?" Jackson asked.

"It's been five years, and I can't see you've learned anything at all," Fiona said.

"You're saying it is hopeless."

"Nothing is hopeless," Fiona said. "It's a miracle we are all here in one piece. It's the holidays. Anything can happen. Maybe we can become friends again. Maybe that will be miracle enough for both of us."

We heard a second truck approaching. This one was Charlie's. Cora met him at the door with a kiss and a hug. "Charlie, can you forgive me?"

"I don't want to look a gift horse in the mouth," Charlie said, "but what have you done that I need to forgive you for?"

"Everything," Cora said. "All our married life, I've felt you were too good to be true. I thought I was losing you for real this time."

Charlie laughed out loud. "Too good to be true, that's a new one. Sorry, honey, you can't get rid of me that easily. It's flattering that you think someone else might want me."

# 26

Before we could sit down, my cell rang. It was Wyatt.

"Sleigh's ready. I called you because I wasn't sure what you wanted me to do next—keep it a secret or let Bob know."

"Bob's right here. You can tell him yourself."

I watched Bob's face light up as Wyatt told him the news.

"How soon can I see it?" he asked. I couldn't hear what Wyatt said, but Bob's smile widened. "Great," he said. "We'll be here. By the way, Wyatt, I need a few minutes with you alone. Can you spare that?"

We didn't hear Wyatt's response.

"Yes," Bob said. "It's an apology, and I am sorry for what happened to your eye."

I believe everyone of us in the room let out a collective breath—an old dog *can* learn new tricks.

Bob hung up the phone and then turned to us. "He's bringing it over, put a new coat of paint on it." He walked over to Albert and sat beside him. "We need to have a long talk—several."

Albert didn't say a word, but he nodded in Bob's direction.

Jackson stood near the door to the hallway. "I'm sorry, Bob," he said. "I never meant for you to get hurt. You gonna call the police?"

"Nope. You wanted to keep Fiona from suffering more than she already had. You did it in the stupidest way imaginable, but I can forgive you for that. Can you, Fiona?"

"If you can forgive him, I probably can," Fiona said. "Have you learned anything at all from this escapade, Jackson?"

"Maybe I've learned what you told me years ago. Not to move so fast. To listen to the people around me and not assume I knew what they were thinking or feeling."

"Those are huge lessons," Fiona said. "I'll have to see if you actually can slow down and hear what I want and not what you think I want."

"Isn't Jackson right about one thing?" Maude asked. "Isn't it hard to be with your father here at Christmas? Don't you think about your baby? It's the time I think about my daughter who died of cancer."

"Of course, it's sad. But where else should I be but with friends and family?"

Maude nodded. "And the parade? The parade, the festivities—will they make you sad?"

"They'll make me smile," Fiona said. "To see people happy always makes me smile. I might even ride in the sleigh with you if there's room, Bob. It will be a grand reunion in a town I love."

Wyatt brought the sleigh over in half an hour. It was gorgeous—bright red with swirls of gold painted on the side.

"The runners weren't gold before," Bob said, "with all those curlicues on them."

"Nope, they weren't like that," Wyatt said. "Fiona's been helping me with the sleigh when she didn't need to be with her dad or watching out for you. She made me promise to tell no one she was around. She suggested the decorations and helped me get them right. She said if I was going to fix something, I should always make it better than it was before. It's over the top in my opinion, but Fiona said Christmas was meant to be over the top."

Bob smiled, and the rest of us watched as Bob and Wyatt walked to the edge of Bob's property near the main road. They talked for fifteen minutes, far enough away that I couldn't hear one word of what was said. But that didn't matter. It was a miracle, and if Bob could apologize to Wyatt for what he'd done accidentally, maybe he could start to apologize to Albert for causing him so much misery in his young life.

EVERYTHING STARTED to move quickly the next day.

We had the best time getting ready for the parade. Anise and Fiona could both squeeze into the sleigh with Bob, dressed as his elves. He'd be free to wave at everyone with his good hand, and Anise would drive. Jackson had just come from a lumber camp up north. He knew a guy who knew a guy who could get us four reindeer if we wanted them. They had been trained for a Christmas movie, and we could get them on loan. I was happy to pay for them.

We were all a little dubious about the reindeer. They came several days early, and Anise took them out in the loaded sleigh. They were good as gold.

We decided to have an open house at Bob's after the parade. We could manage fifty kids and their families, and that's what we did.

Maude, Anise and Cora cooked up a storm. Jackson brought over dozens of animal carvings as presents for the children. As it turned out, he whittled in his spare time at his camps and had enough animals to fill Noah's ark. Wyatt supplied the ark. It sat in the hall to welcome families as they entered.

Each child could choose an animal to take home. Charlie was a tinkerer and he brought over whirligigs and wind-up toys. Albert and Kate brought in a dozen small Christmas trees they'd chopped down from a nearby forrest and decorated them with lights and pine cones. They were everywhere in the house.

I felt this side of useless during the preparations. Kate pointed out that I still had my Mrs. Santa outfit from a previous Christmas and she would be happy to run back to Boston and get it for me. I drew the line at that.

Instead, I spent my time writing a story about our adventures, names changed, of course. It was an article that I might get published. I still knew people at the Boston Globe, and some of those people still knew my father. Never miss an opportunity to publicize your success if you're a business person. That's what my father always said.

How I missed him, especially at Christmas, but Fiona was right. There was no better place to be than among friends during the holidays. Light and laughter were a good cure for the blues.

The party was a resounding success with a few surprises.

I saw Kate talking with a man and his family at the party. He wasn't someone I recognized, but Kate certainly did. They hugged and then she spent half an hour with them and their little girl who looked to be about one. Kate picked up the little girl and showed her all the twinkling lights. When the party ended and we were cleaning up, I asked who the man was.

"Ned. Ned Thompson," she said.

"The one who got away?"

"Yes and no. I worried about running into him in Menescotta. I didn't know how I'd feel. And then I saw him with his family." Kate turned to me with a genuinely warm smile. "It was fine, better than fine. His wife and daughter are darling. He looks happier than I've ever seen him, happier than he ever could have been with me."

"What about you?" I asked.

"I turned him down when he asked me to marry him years ago."

"Do you regret that?"

"I wondered about that decision lately. Had I thrown away an opportunity to be happy? To have a family? To settle down?" Kate said. "I loved Ned, more than any other man I'd ever dated, so I had doubts about my decision."

Kate took both my hands.

"That's why I asked if you were satisfied with your life, if you had any regrets. But that wasn't fair to either one of us. I'm not you."

"Definitely not," I said. "If I had your looks I'd probably have been married five times instead of none."

"Not true, Flo. You had your opportunities, but you didn't want to be married or settle down. Maybe I don't either. I don't know. I'll have to see about that. But I have no regrets about Ned. We would have been a disaster together. I love Menescotta, but I'm not a small-town girl. I could never have been happy with the life his wife seems to love. He was right. He waited to find a woman who wanted the life he could provide, and that wasn't me. Never will be."

Kate dropped my hands and disappeared into the kitchen. She returned with two glasses. "Eggnog with the proper amount of rum." She handed one to me and we clinked our glasses.

"Here's to more adventures, Flo. We can have them whether or not I decide to settle down with someone. You won't kick me out of ODPA if I get married, will you?"

"Of course not, and in a few years you'll be old enough to become a full-fledged member."

She laughed at that.

"Do you have someone in mind?" I asked. "I mean as a potential marriage partner?"

"I'm not sure about that. I've been running so hard from commitment, that it may take me a while to stop running and think about what it is I really want. You'll be the second to know."

"Meaning you'll tell Maude first?" I asked, trying to squash that bit of jealousy that still bubbled up from time to time when people sang Maude's praises.

"Of course not. I'll tell you both together. Once I know."

It was only a few days until Christmas and Cora insisted we stay on. An unexpected storm convinced us that was a good idea. We had a white Christmas, the kind I love, and everything sparkled inside and out. I woke early Christmas Day. No surprise since I wake early every day.

But I wasn't the first person up. I saw Jackson and Fiona in the front yard of Cora and Charlie's house. They must have walked from Bob's place since that's where they were when the storm struck. Now, it was calm. They weren't holding hands, but they were standing very close together, decorating a tree in the yard. I assume that was to be a surprise for all of us. I watched as Jackson tromped from the house to the tree leaving distinct foot prints as if Santa had just left by the front door and not the chimney.

When they were finished, they looked at each other and laughed. I couldn't hear a thing, but I saw how they looked at each other, and I saw them kiss. And I felt right then, for this precious moment, that all was right with the world.

THE END

## FACT VERSUS FICTION

Those of you who know Maine will recognize that Menescotta is a thinly disguised and fictionalized version of the town of Damariscotta. It's a Maine town near Boothbay Harbor that I've loved ever since I stumbled upon it one October. More than a dozen giant pumpkins adorned the sidewalk in front of businesses. They were outrageously decorated and I couldn't wait to visit again. I knew then that the town belonged in a book, but I thought perhaps people in Damariscotta might not like the idea of a would-be murderer roaming their streets, so I changed a few details including the name.

If you don't know Damariscotta, you should. Look it up and plan a visit. You can stop by Portland, Maine, on your way.

## SIGN UP FOR SARAH'S MONTHLY NEWSLETTER

Sign up for my newsletter at:

https://landing.mailerlite.com/webforms/landing/m4w0h9

It includes info on my latest books, tips on writing and research, a favorite recipe, a little humor and more.

## ABOUT THE AUTHOR

Sarah Osborne is the pen name for a writer and physician who has lived all over the United States and loves every part of it. She grew up in northern California, graduated from Oberlin College in Ohio and later got her MD degree from Emory University in Georgia. She lived and worked in Atlanta for many years before moving to Cape Cod.

She writes cozy mysteries for the same reasons she reads them. In a cozy, everything turns out the way it should. The real world can be challenging at times, but in her writing she can make sure the good guys win without too much anxiety along the way.

Her Flo and Maude Christmas Cozies are meant to give women of a certain age the credit they deserve, as well as provide a break for anyone who has too much to do during the holiday season. Visit her at her website: doctorosborne.com and her Facebook page: Sarah Osborne, Mystery Author

Made in the USA
Coppell, TX
19 October 2022